The Loud House

Love Out Loud

PAPERCUTZ
New York

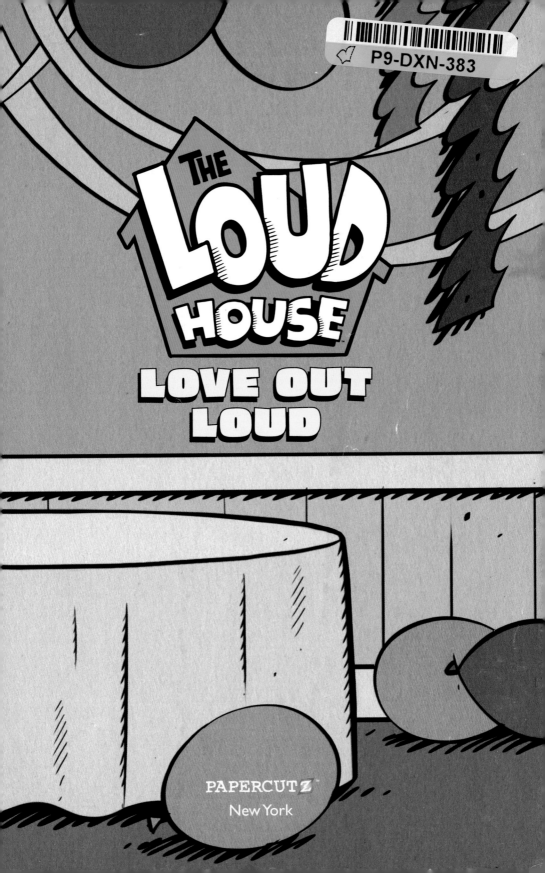

nickelodeon GRAPHIC NOVELS AVAILABLE FROM PAPERCUTZ

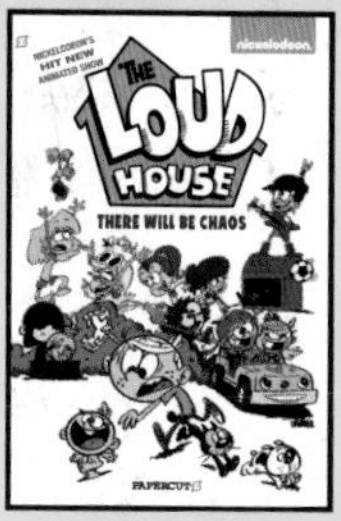
THE LOUD HOUSE
THERE WILL BE CHAOS
THE LOUD HOUSE
#1
"There Will Be Chaos"

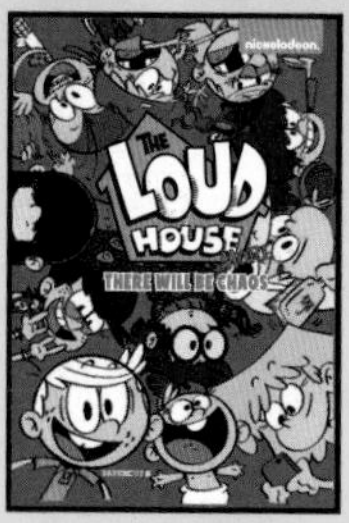
THE LOUD HOUSE
THERE WILL BE CHAOS
THE LOUD HOUSE
#2
"There Will Be More Chaos"

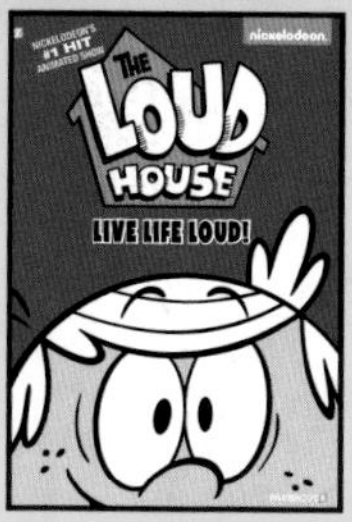
THE LOUD HOUSE
LIVE LIFE LOUD!
THE LOUD HOUSE
#3
"Live Life Loud!"

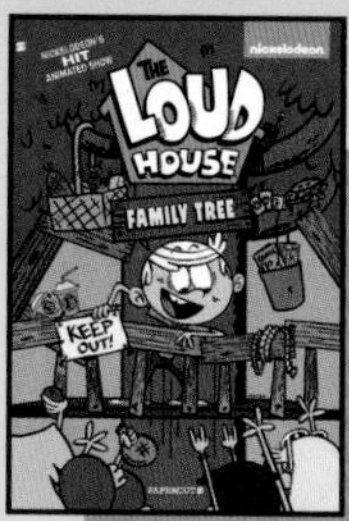
THE LOUD HOUSE
FAMILY TREE
KEEP OUT!
THE LOUD HOUSE
#4
"Family Tree"

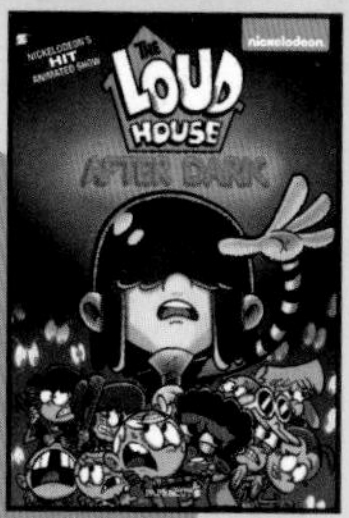
THE LOUD HOUSE
AFTER DARK
THE LOUD HOUSE
#5
"After Dark"

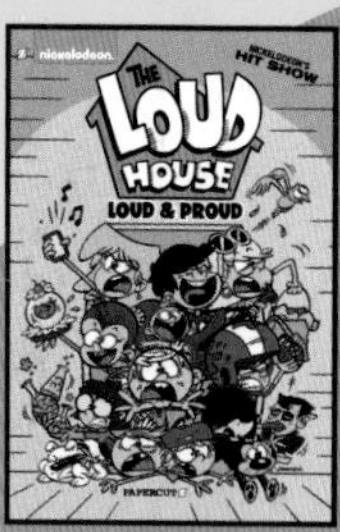
THE LOUD HOUSE
LOUD & PROUD
THE LOUD HOUSE
#6
"Loud and Proud"

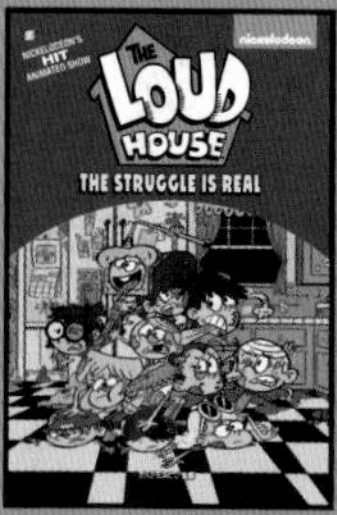
THE LOUD HOUSE
THE STRUGGLE IS REAL
THE LOUD HOUSE
#7
"The Struggle is Real"

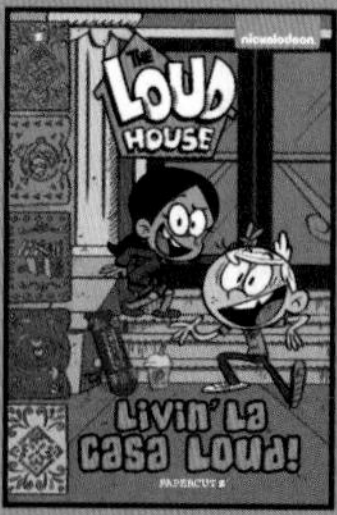
THE LOUD HOUSE
LIVIN' LA CASA LOUD!
THE LOUD HOUSE
#8
"Livin' La Casa Loud"

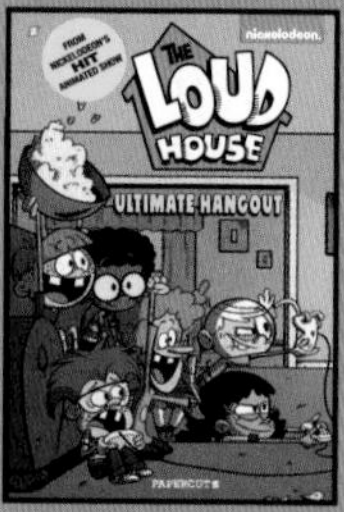
THE LOUD HOUSE
ULTIMATE HANGOUT
THE LOUD HOUSE
#9
"Ultimate Hangout"

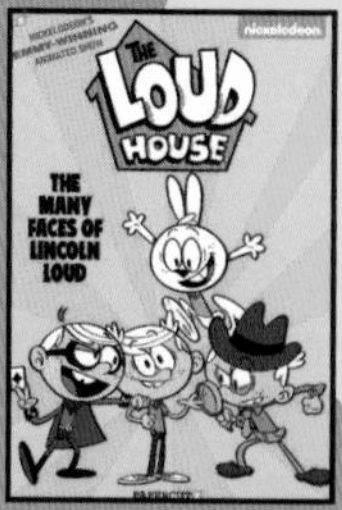
THE LOUD HOUSE
THE MANY FACES OF LINCOLN LOUD
THE LOUD HOUSE
#10
"The Many Faces of Lincoln Loud"

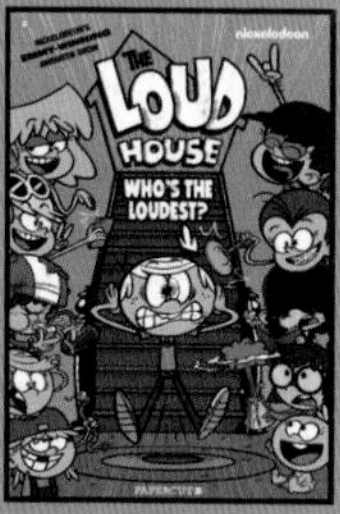
THE LOUD HOUSE
WHO'S THE LOUDEST?
THE LOUD HOUSE
#11
"Who's the Loudest?"

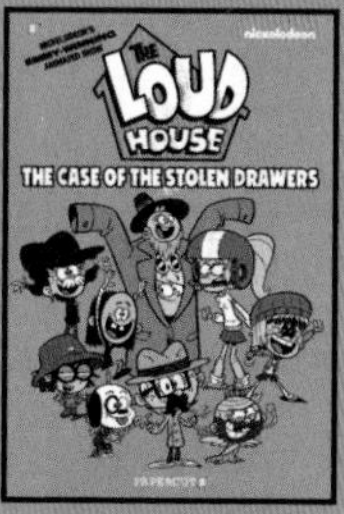
THE LOUD HOUSE
THE CASE OF THE STOLEN DRAWERS
THE LOUD HOUSE
#12
"The Case of the Stolen Drawers"

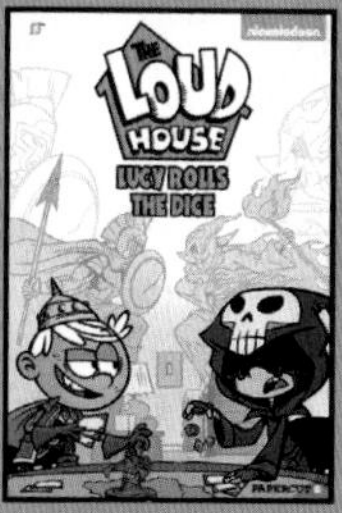
THE LOUD HOUSE
LUCY ROLLS THE DICE
THE LOUD HOUSE
#13
"Lucy Rolls the Dice"

COMING SOON

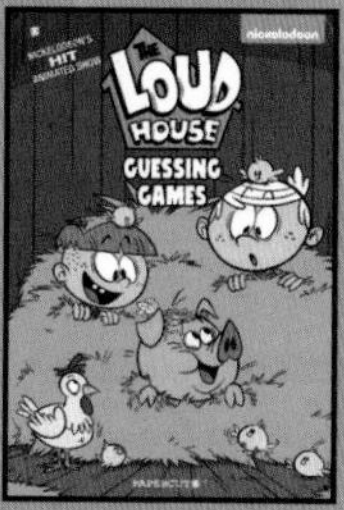
THE LOUD HOUSE
GUESSING GAMES
THE LOUD HOUSE
#14
"Guessing Games"

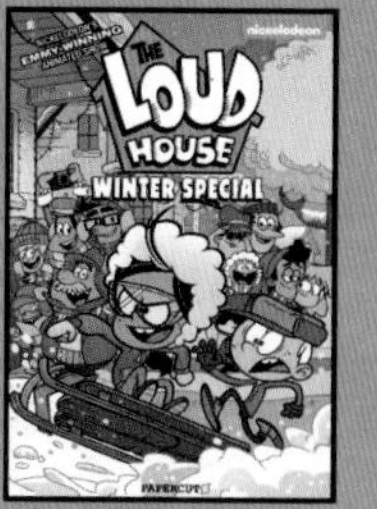
THE LOUD HOUSE
WINTER SPECIAL
THE LOUD HOUSE
WINTER SPECIAL

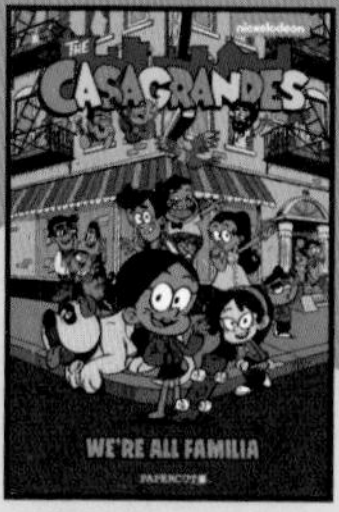
THE CASAGRANDES
WE'RE ALL FAMILIA
THE CASAGRANDES
SPECIAL

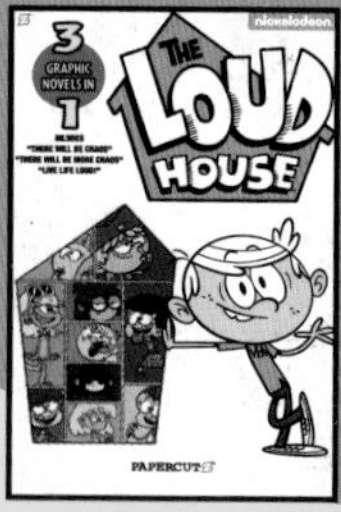
3 GRAPHIC NOVELS IN 1
THE LOUD HOUSE
THE LOUD HOUSE
3 IN 1
#1

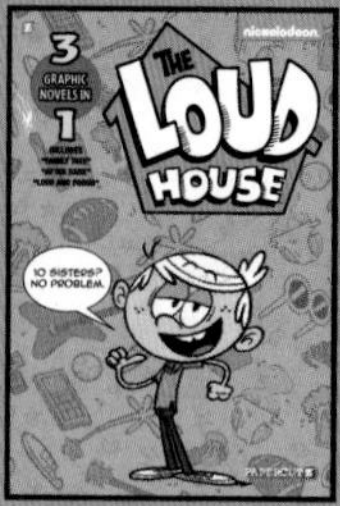
3 GRAPHIC NOVELS IN 1
THE LOUD HOUSE
10 SISTERS? NO PROBLEM.
THE LOUD HOUSE
3 IN 1
#2

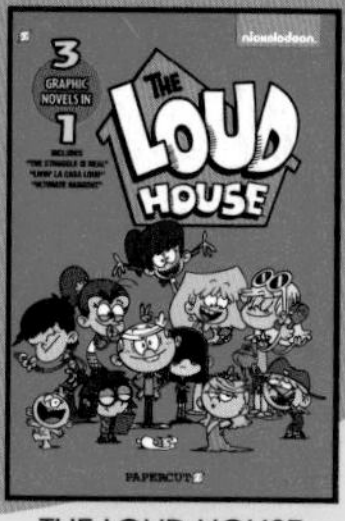
3 GRAPHIC NOVELS IN 1
THE LOUD HOUSE
THE LOUD HOUSE
3 IN 1
#3

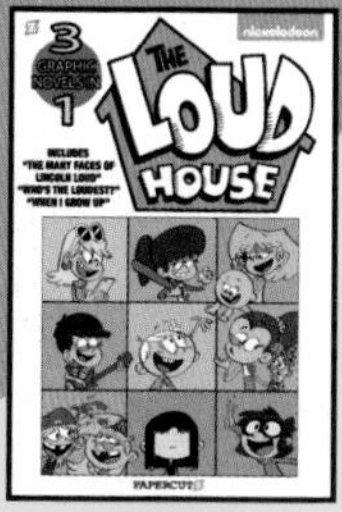
3 GRAPHIC NOVELS IN 1
THE LOUD HOUSE
THE LOUD HOUSE
3 IN 1
#4

The Loud House and The Casagrandes graphic novels and specials are available for $7.99 each in paperback, $12.99 each in hardcover. THE LOUD HOUSE 3 IN 1 graphic novels are available for $14.99 each in paperback only. Available from booksellers everywhere. You can also order online from Papercutz.com, or call 1-800-886-1223, Monday through Friday, 9-5 EST. MC, Visa, and AmEx accepted. To order by mail, please add $5.00 for postage and handling for the first book ordered, $1.00 for each additional book and make check payable to NBM Publishing. Send to: Papercutz, 160 Broadway, Suite 700, East Wing, New York, NY 10038.

Nickelodeon graphic novels are also available digitally wherever e-books are sold.

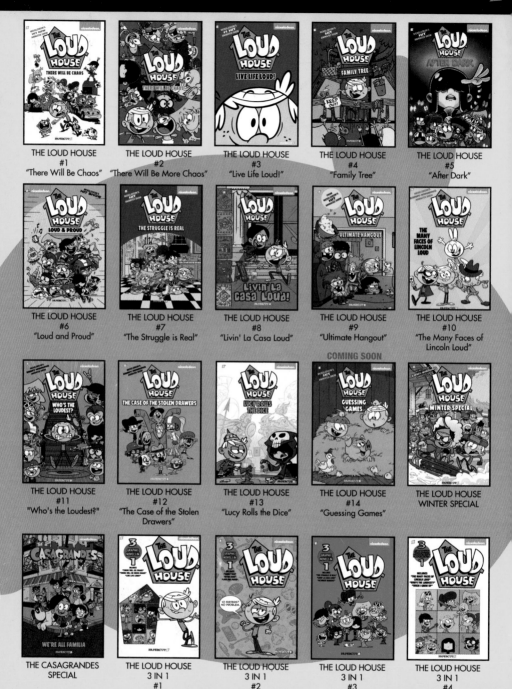

THE LOUD HOUSE

LOVE OUT LOUD

nickelodeon™ THE LOUD HOUSE

LOVE OUT LOUD

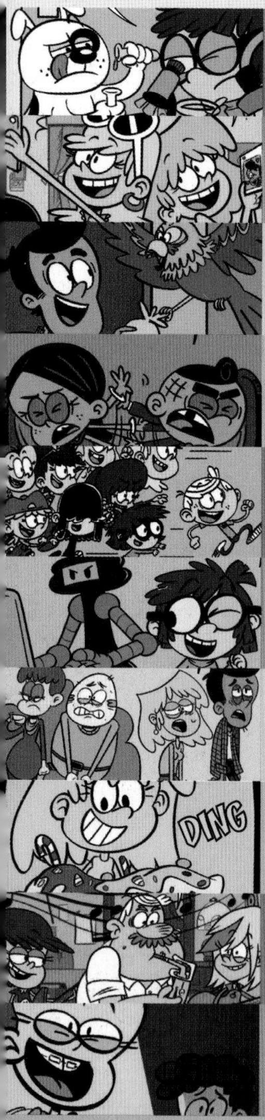
DING

"PUPPY LOVE"
Kiernan Sjursen-Lien — Writer
D.K. Terrell — Artist, Colorist
Wilson Ramos Jr. — Letterer

"SIR RIBBIT"
Rebecca E. Banks — Writer
Amanda Tran — Artist, Colorist
Wilson Ramos Jr. — Letterer

"SIBLING APPRECIATION DAY"
Kara Fein — Writer
Zazo Aguiar— Artist, Colorist
Wilson Ramos Jr. — Letterer

"TIME TO RHYME"
Kiernan Sjursen-Lien — Writer
Amanda Tran — Artist, Colorist
Wilson Ramos Jr. — Letterer

"TWEETHEARTS"
Jair Holguin — Writer
Daniela Rodriguez — Artist, Colorist
Wilson Ramos Jr. — Letterer

"HAPPY PLAN-IVERSARY"
Kara Fein— Writer
Erin Hyde — Artist, Colorist
Wilson Ramos Jr. — Letterer

"WHAT'S LOVE GOT TO DO WITH IT?"
Paloma Uribe — Writer
Amanda Tran — Artist, Colorist
Wilson Ramos Jr. — Letterer

"BEAR HUG"
Amanda Fein — Writer
Daniela Rodriguez — Artist, Colorist
Wilson Ramos Jr. — Letterer

"CUPID'S WINGS"
Kara Fein — Writer
Melissa Kleynowski— Artist
Amanda Tran — Colorist
Wilson Ramos Jr. — Letterer

"BOA ON BOARD"
Amanda Fein — Writer
Zazo Aguiar — Penciller, Colorist
Karolyn Rocha — Inker
Wilson Ramos Jr. — Letterer

"FOR THE LOVE OF THE GAME"
Amanda Fein — Writer
D.K. Terrell — Artist, Colorist
Wilson Ramos Jr. — Letterer

"CAFÉ CONFUSION"
Caitlin Fein — Writer
Max Alley — Artist
Peter Bertucci — Colorist
Wilson Ramos Jr. — Letterer

"OVER THE LINE"
Amanda Fein — Writer
Shannon Parayil — Artist, Colorist
Wilson Ramos Jr. — Letterer

"MANIC MONDAY"
Jair Holguin — Writer
Lena Bishop — Layout Artist
Melissa Kleynowski — Inker
Efrain Rodriguez — Colorist
Wilson Ramos Jr. — Letterer

"MADE WITH CARE"
Derek Fridolfs — Writer
D.K. Terrell — Artist, Colorist
Wilson Ramos Jr. — Letterer

"FROM THE HEART"
Kara Fein — Writer
Melissa Kleynowski — Artist
Efrain Rodriguez — Colorist
Wilson Ramos Jr. — Letterer

"SENIOR PROM"
Amanda Fein — Writer
Zazo Aguiar — Penciller, Colorist
Karolyn Rocha — Inker
Wilson Ramos Jr. — Letterer

"THERE'S SOMETHING ABOUT LALO"
Amanda Fein — Writer
Jennifer Hernandez — Artist, Colorist
Wilson Ramos Jr. — Letterer

"O-PUN-ING NIGHT"
Jair Holguin — Writer
Michelle Hiraishi — Artist, Colorist
Wilson Ramos Jr. — Letterer

"FRIENDIVERSARY"
Jair Holguin — Writer
Erin Hyde — Artist, Colorist
Wilson Ramos Jr. — Letterer

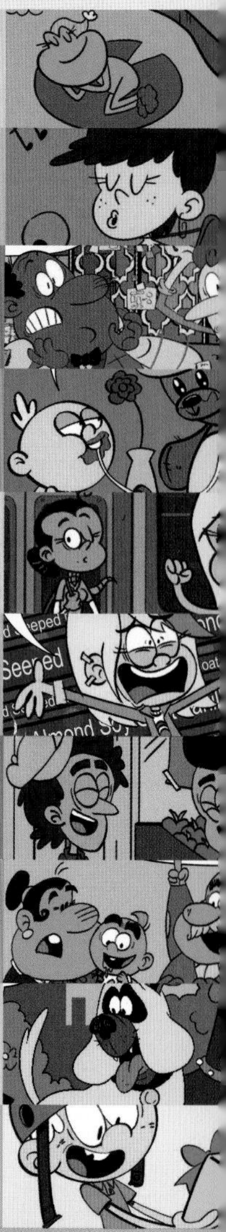

TYLER KOBERSTEIN — Cover Artist
JORDAN ROSATO — Endpapers
JAMES SALERNO — Sr. Art Director/Nickelodeon
JAYJAY JACKSON — Design
EMMA BONE, CAITLIN FEIN, KRISTEN G. SMITH, NEIL WADE, DANA CLUVERIUS, MOLLIE FREILICH — Special Thanks
JORDAN HILLMAN — Editorial Intern
JEFF WHITMAN — Editor
JOAN HILTY — Comics Editor/Nickelodeon
JIM SALICRUP
Editor-in-Chief

ISBN: 978-1-5458-0854-2 paperback edition
ISBN: 978-1-5458-0853-5 hardcover edition

www.papercutz.com

Papercutz books may be purchased for business or promotional use. For information on bulk purchases please contact Macmillan Corporate and Premium Sales Department at (800) 221-7945 x5442.

Printed in Turkey
December 2021

Distributed by Macmillan
First Printing

MEET THE LOUD FAMILY *and friends!*

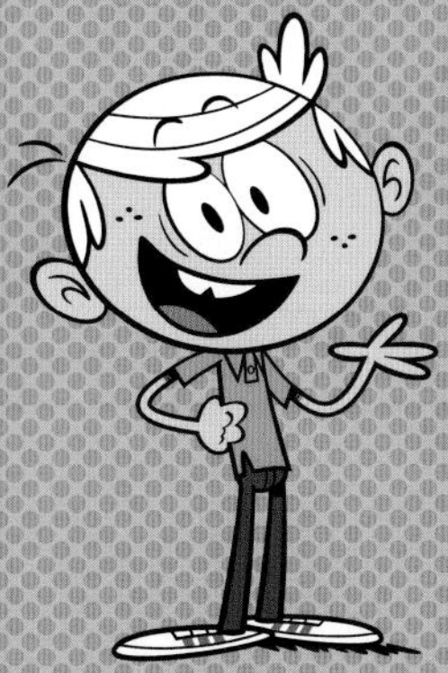

LINCOLN LOUD
THE MIDDLE CHILD

Lincoln is the middle child, with five older sisters and five younger sisters. He has learned that surviving the Loud household means staying a step ahead. He's the man with a plan, always coming up with a way to get what he wants or deal with a problem, even if things inevitably go wrong. Being the only boy comes with some perks. Lincoln gets his own room – even if it's just a converted linen closet. On the other hand, being the only boy also means he sometimes gets a little too much attention from his sisters. They mother him, tease him, and use him as the occasional lab rat or fashion show participant. Lincoln's sisters may drive him crazy, but he loves them and is always willing to help out if they need him.

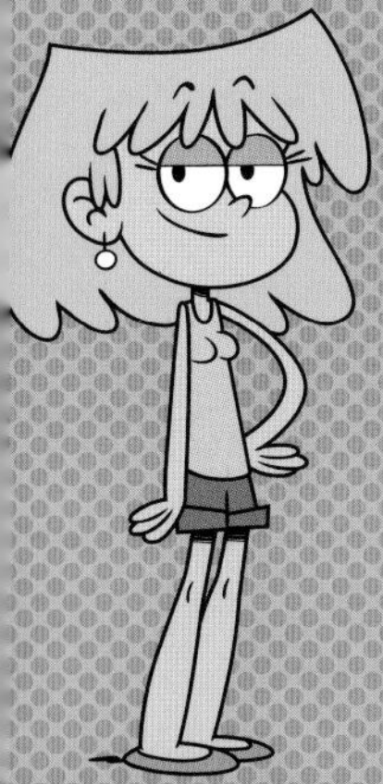

LORI LOUD
THE OLDEST

As the first-born child of the Loud Clan, Lori sees herself as the boss of all her siblings. She feels she's paved the way for them and deserves extra respect. Her signature traits are rolling her eyes, texting her boyfriend, Bobby, and literally saying "literally" all the time. Because she's the oldest and most experienced sibling, Lori can be a great ally, so it pays to stay on her good side, especially since she can drive.

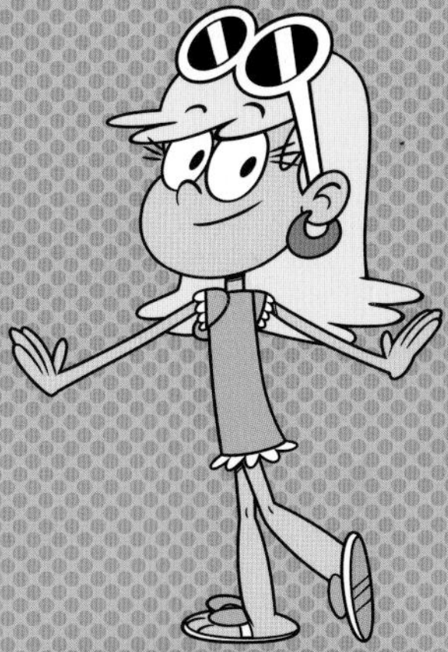

LENI LOUD
THE FASHIONISTA

Leni spends most of her time designing outfits and accessorizing. She always falls for Luan's pranks, and sometimes walks into walls when she's talking (she's not great at doing two things at once). Leni might be flighty, but she's the sweetest of the Loud siblings and truly has a heart of gold (even though she's pretty sure it's a heart of blood).

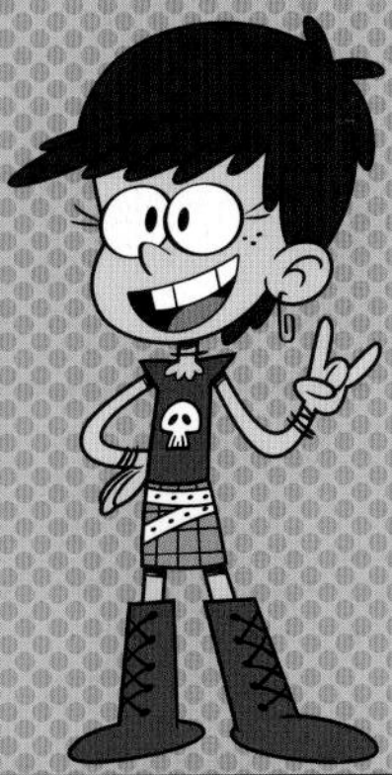

LUNA LOUD
THE ROCK STAR

Luna is loud, boisterous and freewheeling, and her energy is always cranked to 11. She thinks about music so much that she even talks in song lyrics. On the off-chance she doesn't have her guitar with her, everything can and will be turned into a musical instrument. You can always count on Luna to help out, and she'll do most anything you ask, as long as you're okay with her supplying a rocking guitar accompaniment.

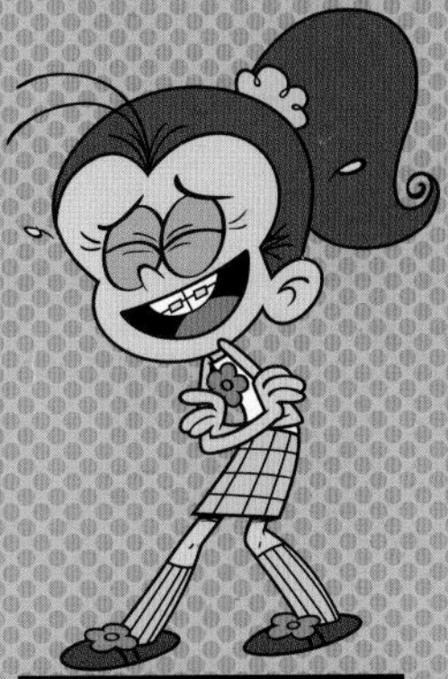

LUAN LOUD
THE JOKESTER

Luan's a standup comedienne who provides a nonstop barrage of silly puns. She's big on prop comedy too – squirting flowers and whoopee cushions – so you have to be on your toes whenever she's around. She loves to pull pranks and is a really good ventriloquist – she is often found doing bits with her dummy, Mr. Coconuts. Luan never lets anything get her down; to her, laughter IS the best medicine.

LYNN LOUD
THE ATHLETE

Lynn is athletic and full of energy and is always looking for a teammate. With her, it's all sports all the time. She'll turn anything into a sport. Putting away eggs? Jump shot! Score! Cleaning up the eggs? Slap shot! Score! Lynn is very competitive, but despite her competitive nature, she always tries to just have a good time.

LUCY LOUD
THE EMO

You can always count on Lucy to give the morbid point of view in any given situation. She is obsessed with all things spooky and dark – funerals, vampires, séances, and the like. She wears mostly black and writes moody poetry. She's usually quiet and keeps to herself. Lucy has a way of mysteriously appearing out of nowhere, and try as they might, her siblings never get used to this.

LOLA LOUD
THE BEAUTY QUEEN

Lola could not be more different from her twin sister, Lana. She's a pageant powerhouse whose interests include glitter, photo shoots, and her own beautiful, beautiful face. But don't let her cute, gap-toothed smile fool you; underneath all the sugar and spice lurks a Machiavellian mastermind. Whatever Lola wants, Lola gets – or else. She's the eyes and ears of the household and never resists an opportunity to tattle on troublemakers. But if you stay on Lola's good side, you've got yourself a fierce ally – and a lifetime supply of free makeovers.

LANA LOUD
THE TOMBOY

Lana is the rough-and-tumble sparkplug counterpart to her twin sister, Lola. She's all about reptiles, mud pies, and muffler repair. She's the resident Ms. Fix-it and is always ready to lend a hand – the dirtier the job, the better. Need your toilet unclogged? Snake fed? Back-zit popped? Lana's your gal. All she asks in return is a little A-B-C gum, or a handful of kibble (she often sneaks it from the dog bowl).

LISA LOUD
THE GENIUS

Lisa is smarter than the rest of her siblings combined. She'll most likely be a rocket scientist, or a brain surgeon, or an evil genius who takes over the world. Lisa spends most of her time working in her lab (the family has gotten used to the explosions), and says her research leaves little time for frivolous human pursuits like "playing" or "getting haircuts." That said, she's always there to help with a homework question, or to explain why the sky is blue, or to point out the structural flaws in someone's pillow fort. Lisa says it's the least she can do for her favorite test subjects, er, siblings.

LILY LOUD
THE BABY

Lily is a giggly, drooly, diaper-ditching free spirit, affectionately known as "the poop machine." You can't keep a nappy on this kid – she's like a teething Houdini. But even when Lily's running wild, dropping rancid diaper bombs, or drooling all over the remote, she always brings a smile to everyone's face (and a clothespin to their nose). Lily is everyone's favorite little buddy, and the whole family loves her unconditionally.

RITA LOUD

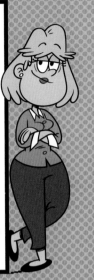

Mother to the eleven Loud kids, Mom (Rita Loud) wears many different hats. She's a chauffeur, homework-checker and barf-cleaner-upper all rolled into one. She's always there for her kids and ready to jump into action during a crisis, whether it's a fight between the twins or Leni's missing shoe. When she's not chasing the kids around or at her day job as a dental hygienist, Mom pursues her passion: writing. She also loves taking on house projects and is very handy with tools (guess that's where Lana gets it from). Between writing, working and being a mom, her days are always hectic but she wouldn't have it any other way.

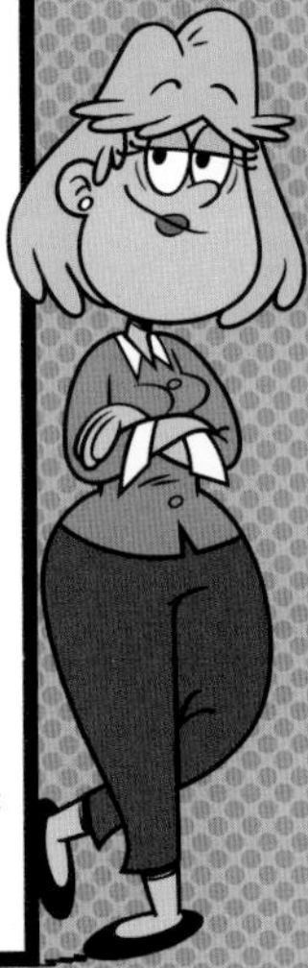

LYNN LOUD SR.

Dad (Lynn Loud Sr.) is a fun-loving, upbeat aspiring chef. A kid-at-heart, he's not above taking part in the kids' zany schemes. In addition to cooking, Dad loves his van, playing the cowbell and making puns. Before meeting Mom, Dad spent a semester in England and has been obsessed with British culture ever since – and sometimes "accidentally" slips into a British accent. When Dad's not wrangling the kids, he's pursuing his dream of opening his own restaurant where he hopes to make his "Lynn-sagnas" world-famous.

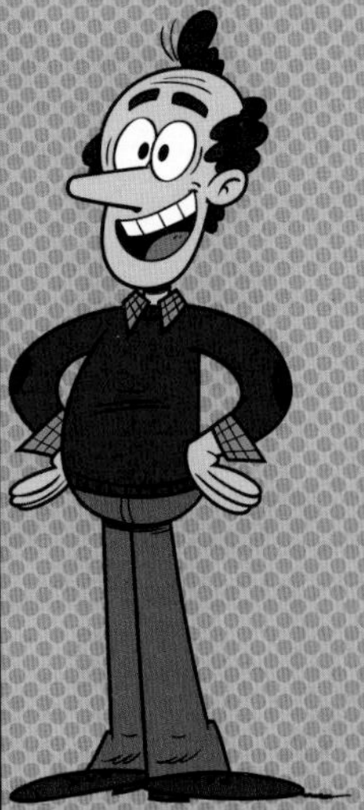

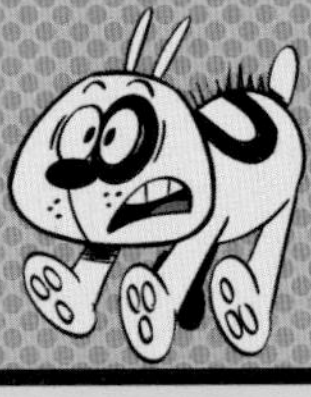

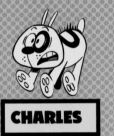

CHARLES

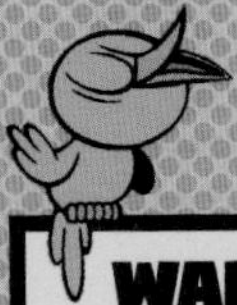

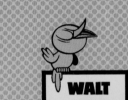

WALT

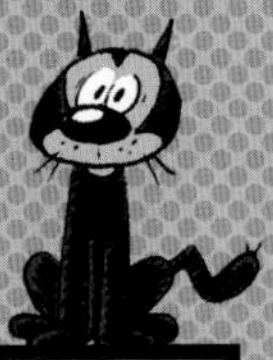

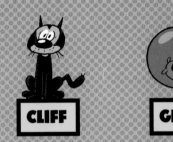

CLIFF

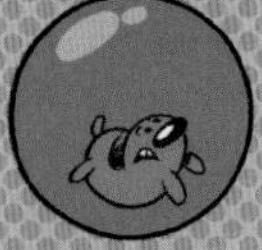

GEO

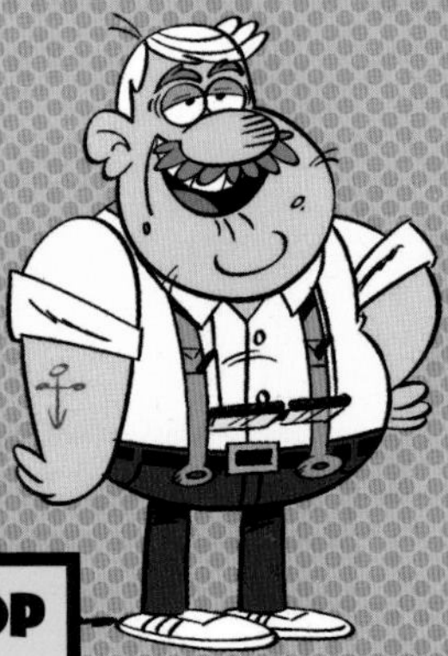

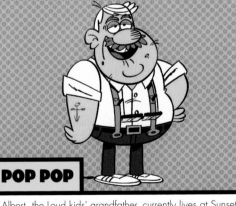

POP POP

Albert, the Loud kids' grandfather, currently lives at Sunset Canyon Retirement Community after dedicating his life to working in the military. Pop Pop spends his days dominating at shuffleboard, eating pudding, and going on adventures with his pals Bernie, Scoots, and Seymour and his girlfriend, Myrtle. Pop Pop is upbeat, fun-loving, and cherishes spending time with his grandchildren.

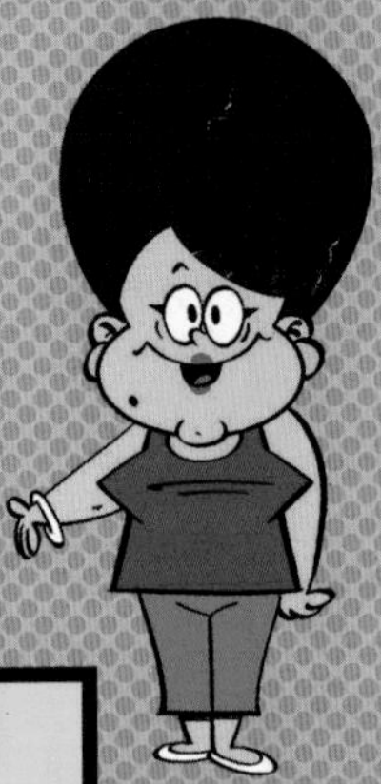

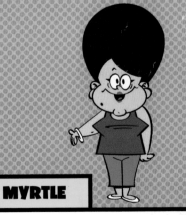

MYRTLE

Myrtle, or Gran-Gran, is Albert's (Pop Pop's) girlfriend. She loves traveling and hanging out with Albert and the Loud kids. Since she doesn't have grandkids of her own, she's the Loud kids' honorary grandma and can't help but smother them with love.

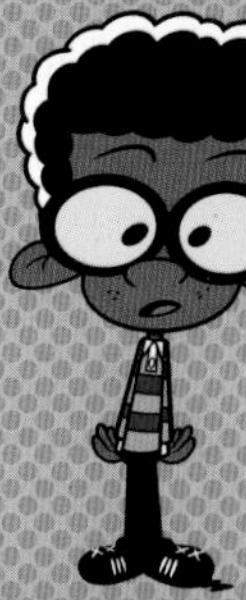

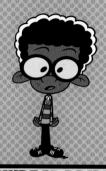

CLYDE McBRIDE
THE BEST FRIEND

Clyde is Lincoln's partner in crime. He's always willing to go along with Lincoln's crazy schemes (even if he sees the flaws in them up-front). Lincoln and Clyde are two peas in a pod and share pretty much all of the same tastes in movies, comics, TV shows, toys—you name it. As an only child, Clyde envies Lincoln—how cool would it be to always have siblings around to talk to? But since Clyde spends so much time at the Loud household, he's almost an honorary sibling anyway.

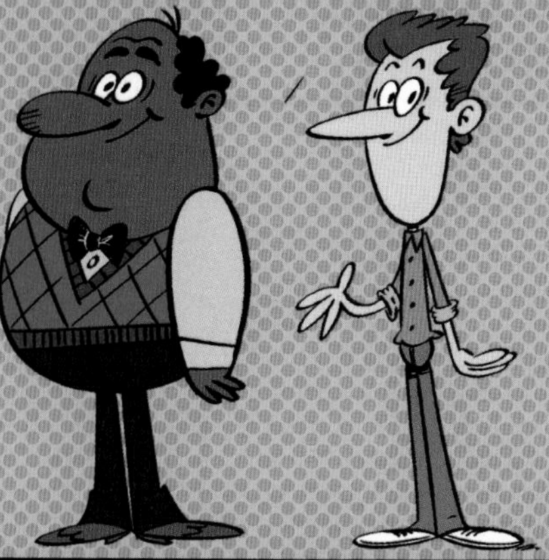

HAROLD AND HOWARD McBRIDE
Clyde's Loving Dads

Harold and Howard are Clyde's loving dads and only want the best for him, but what they define as "the best" may differ. Harold is a level-headed, straight-shooter with a heart of gold. The more easygoing of Clyde's dads, Harold often has to convince Howard that it's okay for them to not constantly hover over Clyde. Howard is an anxious helicopter parent and it's easy for him to break down into emotional sobbing, whether it be sad times (like when Clyde stubbed his toe) or happy (like when Clyde and Lincoln beat that really tough video game boss). Despite their differing parenting styles, the two dads bring nothing but love to the table.

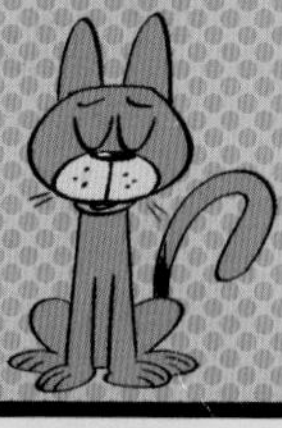

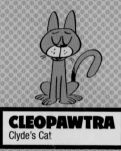

CLEOPAWTRA
Clyde's Cat

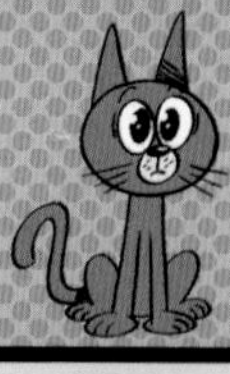

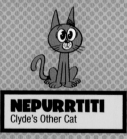

NEPURRTITI
Clyde's Other Cat

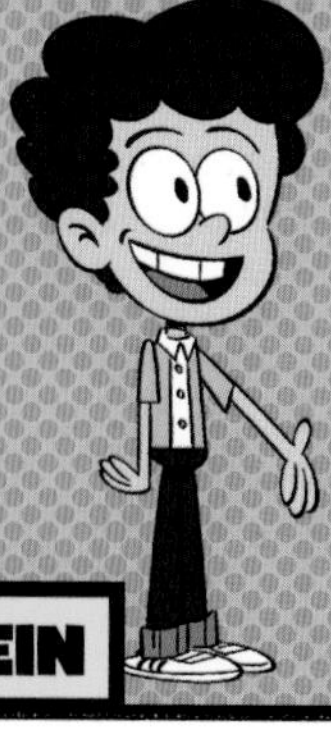

BENNY STEIN

Benny is Luan's classmate, costar, and boyfriend. He's shy and quirky, but also sweet and earnest. He's not a zany comedian like Luan, but he sure enjoys her sense of humor and appreciates her wicked skills when it comes to prop comedy. Luan keeps Benny laughing, and Benny keeps Luan from sweating the small stuff. And as his marionette, Mrs. Appleblossom, would remind him (in her sassy British accent), it's all small stuff.

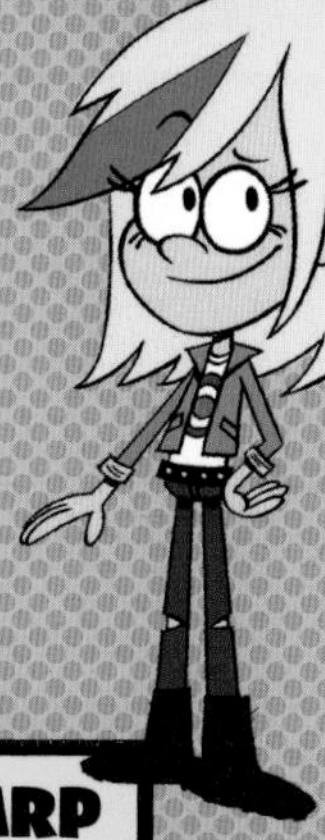

SAM SHARP

Sam is Luna's classmate and good friend, who Luna has a crush on. Sam is all about the music – she loves to play guitar and write and compose music. Her favorite genre is rock and roll but she appreciates all good tunes. Unlike Luna, Sam only has one brother, Simon, but she thinks even one sibling provides enough chaos for her.

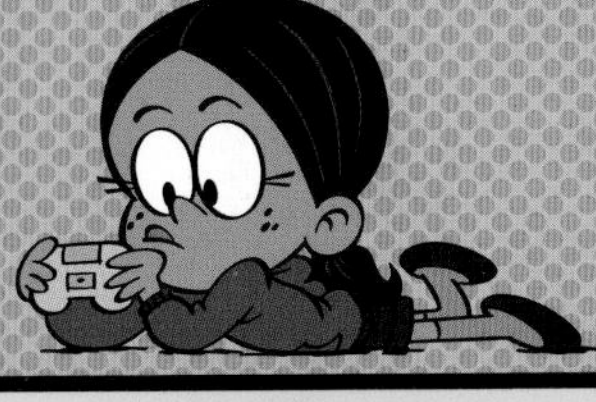

RONNIE ANNE SANTIAGO

Ronnie Anne's a skateboarding city girl now. She's fearless, free-spirited, and always quick to come up with a plan. She's one tough cookie, but she also has a sweet side. Ronnie Anne loves helping her family, and that's taught her to help others, too. When she's not pitching in at the family mercado, you can find her exploring the neighborhood with her best friend Sid, or ordering hot dogs with her skater buds Casey, Nikki, and Sameer.

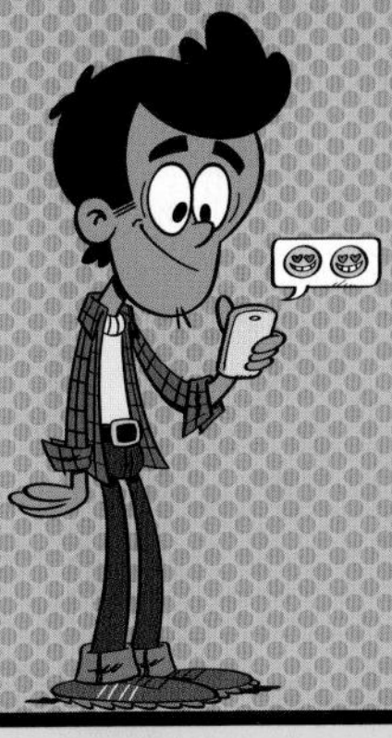

BOBBY SANTIAGO

Bobby is Ronnie Anne's big bro. He's a student and one of the hardest workers in the city! He loves his family and loves working at the Mercado. As his Abuelo's right hand man, Bobby can't wait to take over the family business one day. He's a big kid at heart, and his clumsiness gets him into some sticky situations at work, like locking himself in the freezer. Mercado mishaps aside, everyone in the neighborhood loves to come to the store and talk to Bobby.

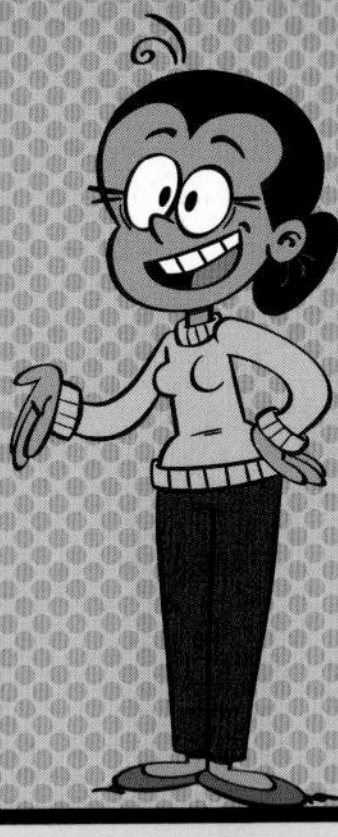

MARIA CASAGRANDE SANTIAGO

She's the mother of Bobby and Ronnie Anne. A hardworking nurse, she doesn't get to spend a lot of time with her kids, but when she does she treasures it. Maria is calm and rational but often worries about whether she's doing enough for her kids. Maria, Bobby, and Ronnie Anne are a close-knit trio who were used to having only each other – until they moved in with their extended family.

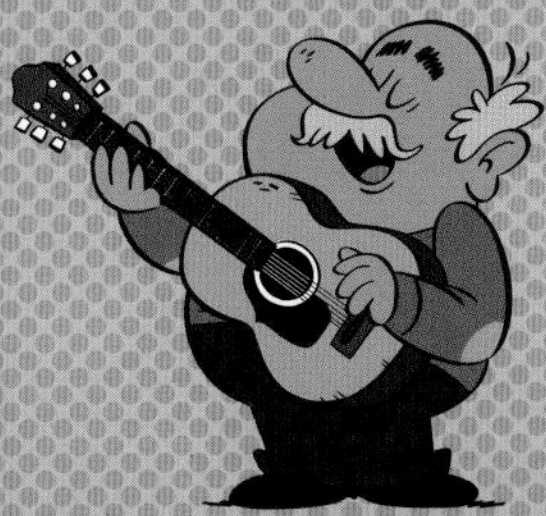

HECTOR CASAGRANDE

Hector is Carlos and Maria's dad, and the Abuelo of the family (that means grandpa)! He owns the Mercado on the ground floor of their apartment building and takes great pride in his work, his family, and being the unofficial "mayor" of the block. He loves to tell stories, share his ideas, and gossip (even though he won't admit to it). You can find him working in the Mercado, playing guitar, or watching his favorite telenovela.

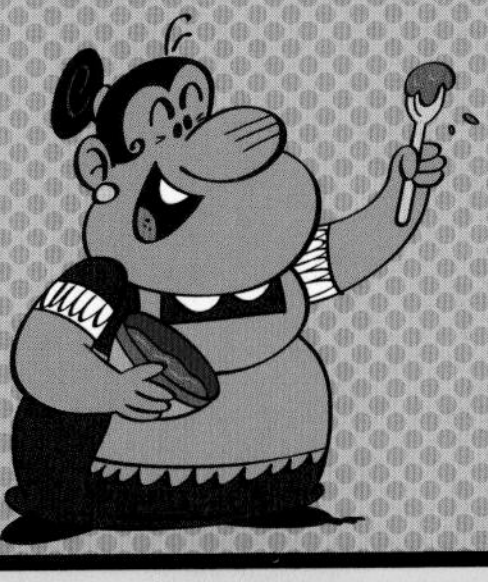

ROSA CASAGRANDE

Rosa is Carlos and Maria's mom and the Abuela of the family (that means grandma)! She's the head of the household, the wisest Casagrande, and the master cook with a superhuman ability to tell when anyone in the house is hungry. She often tries to fix problems or illnesses with traditional Mexican home remedies and potions. She's very protective of her family… sometimes a little too much.

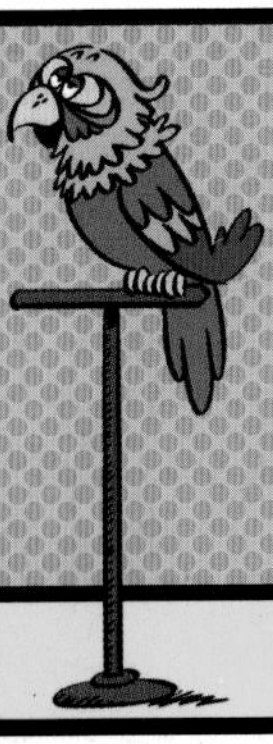

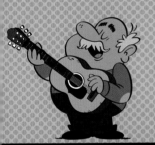

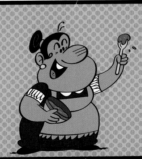

SERGIO

Sergio is the Casagrandes' beloved pet parrot. He's a blunt, sassy bird who "thinks" he's full of wisdom and always has something to say. The Casagrandes have to keep a close eye on their credit card as Sergio is addicted to online shopping and is always asking the family to buy him some new gadget he saw on TV. Sergio is most loyal to Rosa and serves as her wing-man, partner in crime, taste tester, and confidant. He can be found trying to get his ex-girlfriend, Priscilla (an ostrich at the zoo), to respond to him.

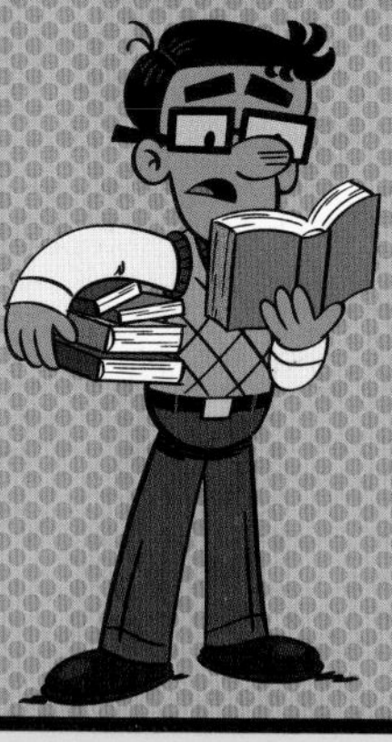

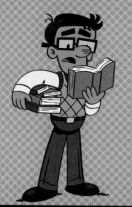

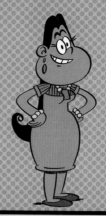

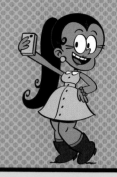

CARLOS CASAGRANDE

Carlos is Maria's brother. He's married to Frida, and together they have four kids: Carlota, C.J., Carl, and Carlitos. Carlos is a Professor of Cultural Studies at a local college. Usually he has his heads in the clouds or his nose in a textbook. Relatively easygoing, Carlos is a loving father and an enthusiastic teacher who tries to get his kids interested in their Mexican heritage.

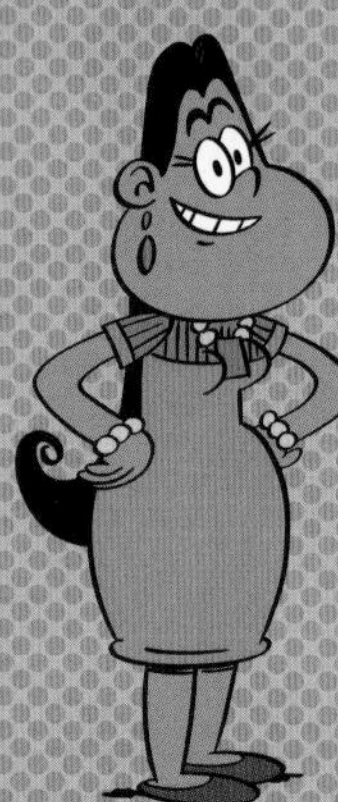

FRIDA PUGA CASAGRANDE

Frida is Carlos, C.J., Carl, and Carlitos' mom. She's an art professor and a performance artist, and is always looking for new ways to express herself. She's got a big heart and isn't shy about her emotions. Frida tends to cry when she's sad, happy, angry, or any other emotion you can think of. She's always up for fun, is passionate about her art, and loves her family more than anything.

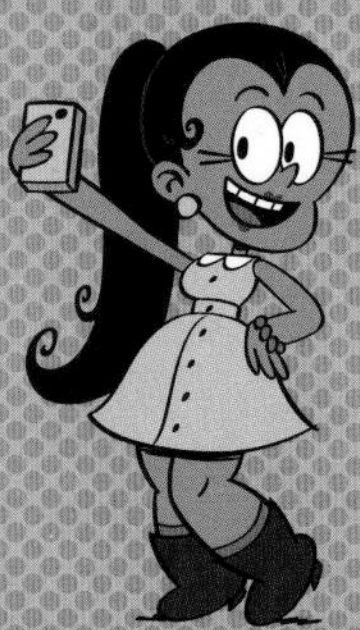

CARLOTA CASAGRANDE

Carlota is CJ, Carl, and Carlitos' older sister. A social media influencer, she's excited to be like a big sister to Ronnie Anne. She's a force to be reckoned with, and is always trying to share her distinctive vintage style tips with Ronnie Anne.

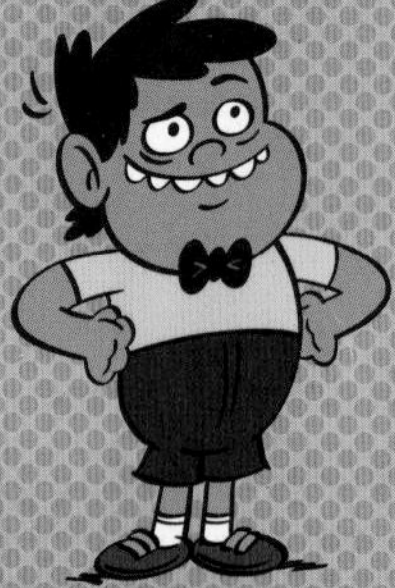

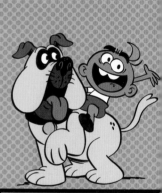

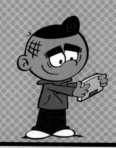

CJ (CARLOS JR.) CASAGRANDE

CJ is Carlota's younger brother and Carl and Carlitos' older brother. He was born with Down Syndrome. He lights up any room with his infectious smile and is always ready to play. He's obsessed with pirates and is BFFs with Bobby. He likes to wear a bowtie to any family occasion, and you can always catch him laughing or helping his *abuela*.

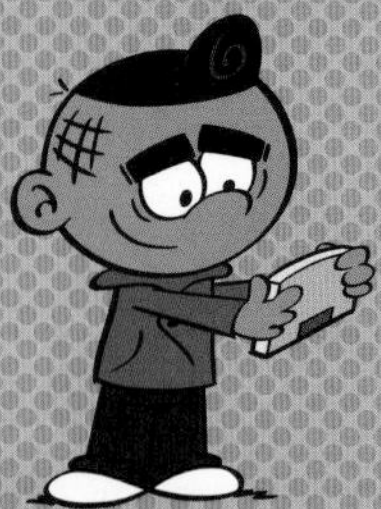

CARL CASAGRANDE

Carl is wise beyond his years. He's confident, outgoing, and puts a lot of time and effort into looking good. He likes to think of himself as a suave businessman and doesn't like to get caught playing with his action figures or wearing his footie PJs. Even though Bobby is nothing but nice to him, Carl sees his big cousin as his biggest rival.

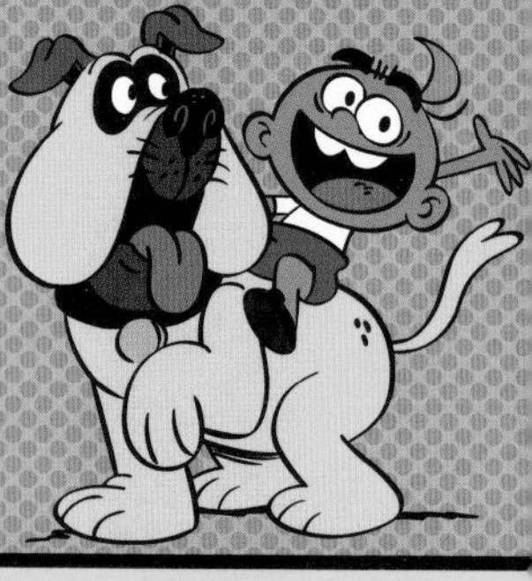

CARLITOS CASAGRANDE

Carlitos is the baby of the family, and is always copying the behavior of everyone in the household—even if they aren't human. He's a playful and silly baby who loves to play with the family pets.

LALO

Lalo is a slobbery bull mastiff who thinks he's a lapdog. He's not the smartest pup, and gets scared easily... but he loves his family and loves to cuddle.

STANLEY CHANG

Stanley Chang is Sid's dad. He's a conductor on the GLART-train that runs through the city. He's a patient man who likes to do Tai Chi when he gets stressed out. He likes to cheer up train commuters with fun facts, but emotionally he breaks down more than the train does.

BECCA CHANG

Becca Chang is Sid's mom. Like her daughter, Becca is quirky, smart, and funny. She works at the Great Lakes City Zoo and often brings her work home with her, which means the Chang household can also be a bit of a zoo.

ADELAIDE CHANG

Adelaide Chang is Sid's little sister. She's 6 years old, and has a flair for the dramatic. You can always find her trying to make her way into her big sister Sid's adventures.

FROGGY 2

SID CHANG

Sid is Ronnie Anne's quirky best friend. She's new to the city but dives head-first into everything she finds interesting. She and her family just moved into the apartment one floor above the Casagrandes. In fact, Sid's bedroom is right above Ronnie Anne's! A dream come true for any BFFs.

MAYBELLE

Maybelle is a cranky neighborhood regular at the *Mercado* who is obsessed with mangoes. They might be the only thing she eats! Her other loves include movie heartthrob Javier Luna and a good deal. Maybelle is very picky and never misses a chance to complain, but the Casagrandes love her dearly.

"PUPPY LOVE"

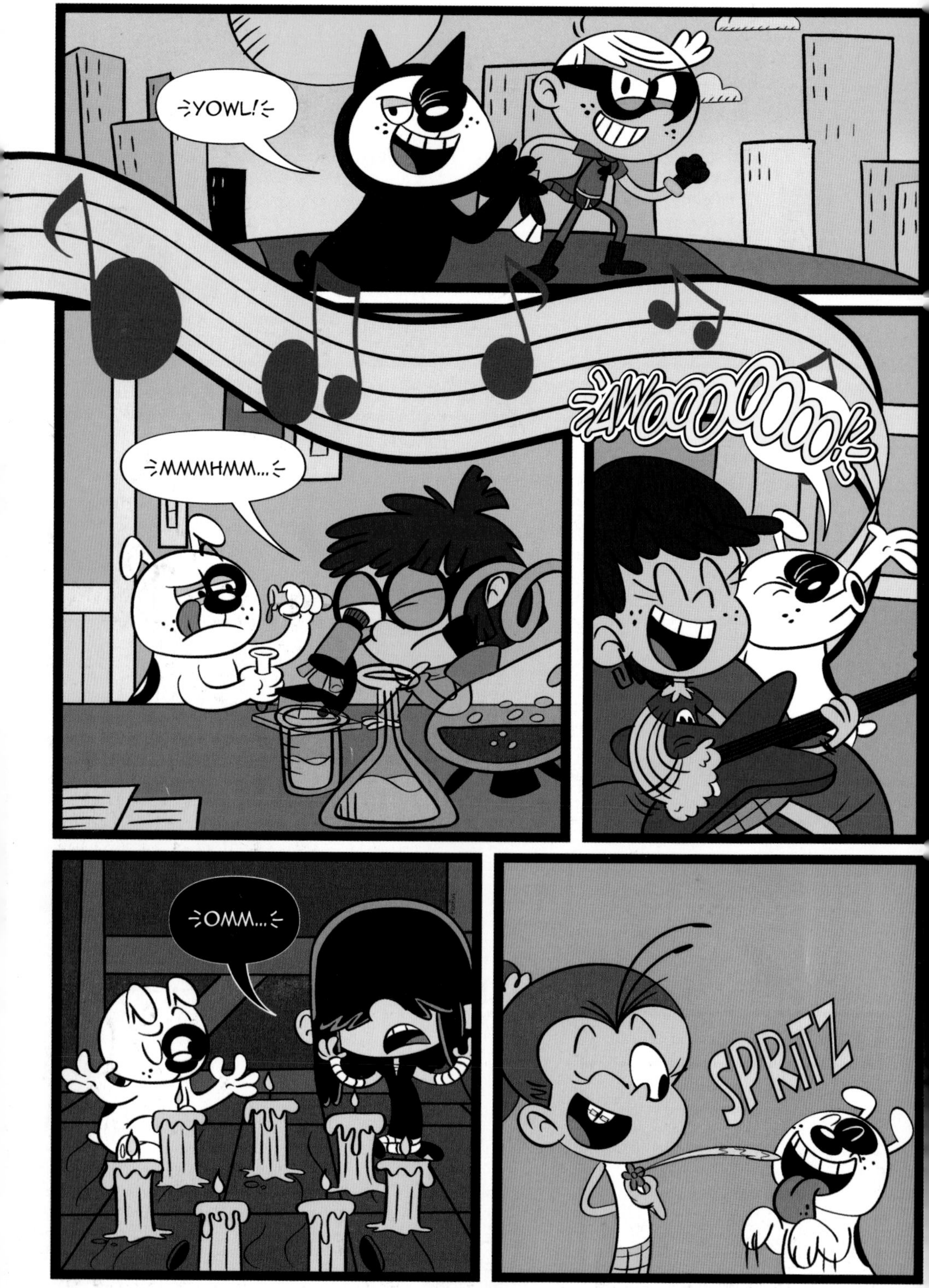
YOWL!
MMMHMM...
AWOOOOOOOO!
OMM...
SPRITZ

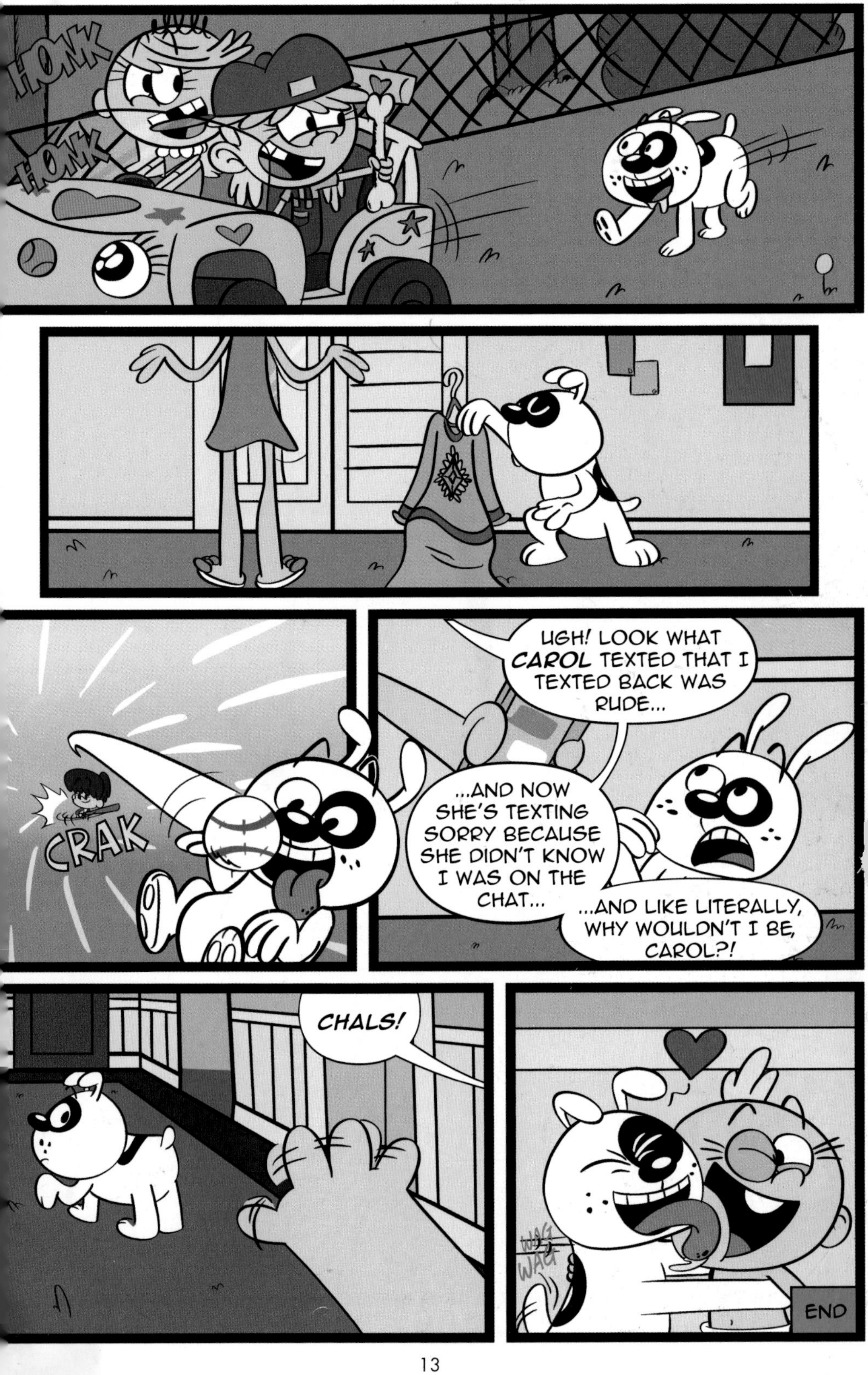
HONK
HONK
CRAK
UGH! LOOK WHAT CAROL TEXTED THAT I TEXTED BACK WAS RUDE...
...AND NOW SHE'S TEXTING SORRY BECAUSE SHE DIDN'T KNOW I WAS ON THE CHAT...
...AND LIKE LITERALLY, WHY WOULDN'T I BE, CAROL?!
CHALS!
WAG
WAG
END

"SIBLING APPRECIATION DAY"

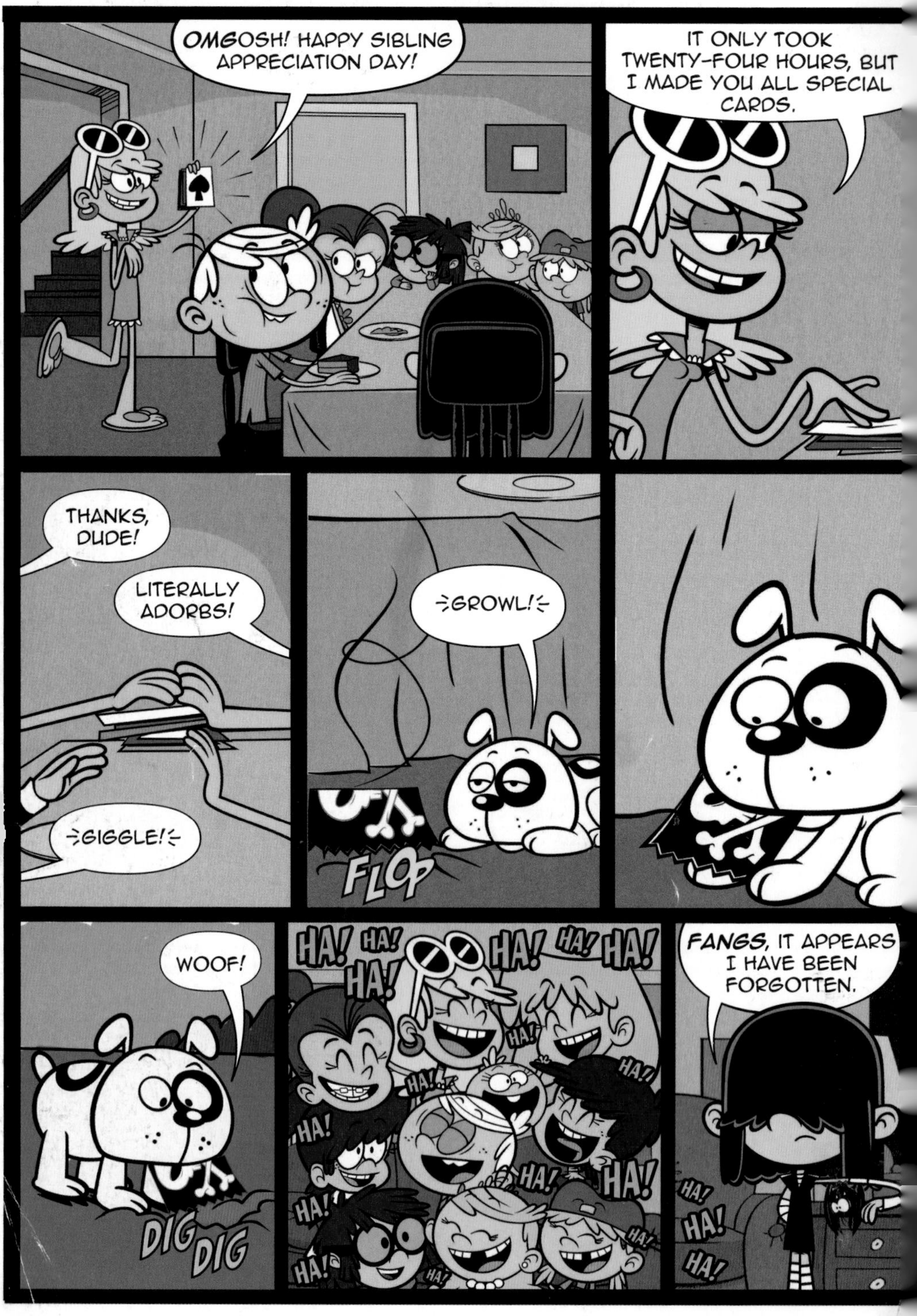
OMGOSH! HAPPY SIBLING APPRECIATION DAY!
IT ONLY TOOK TWENTY-FOUR HOURS, BUT I MADE YOU ALL SPECIAL CARDS.
THANKS, DUDE!
LITERALLY ADORBS!
GIGGLE!
GROWL!
FLOP
WOOF!
DIG DIG
HA! HA! HA! HA! HA! HA!
HA! HA! HA! HA! HA! HA! HA! HA!
FANGS, IT APPEARS I HAVE BEEN FORGOTTEN.
HA! HA! HA!

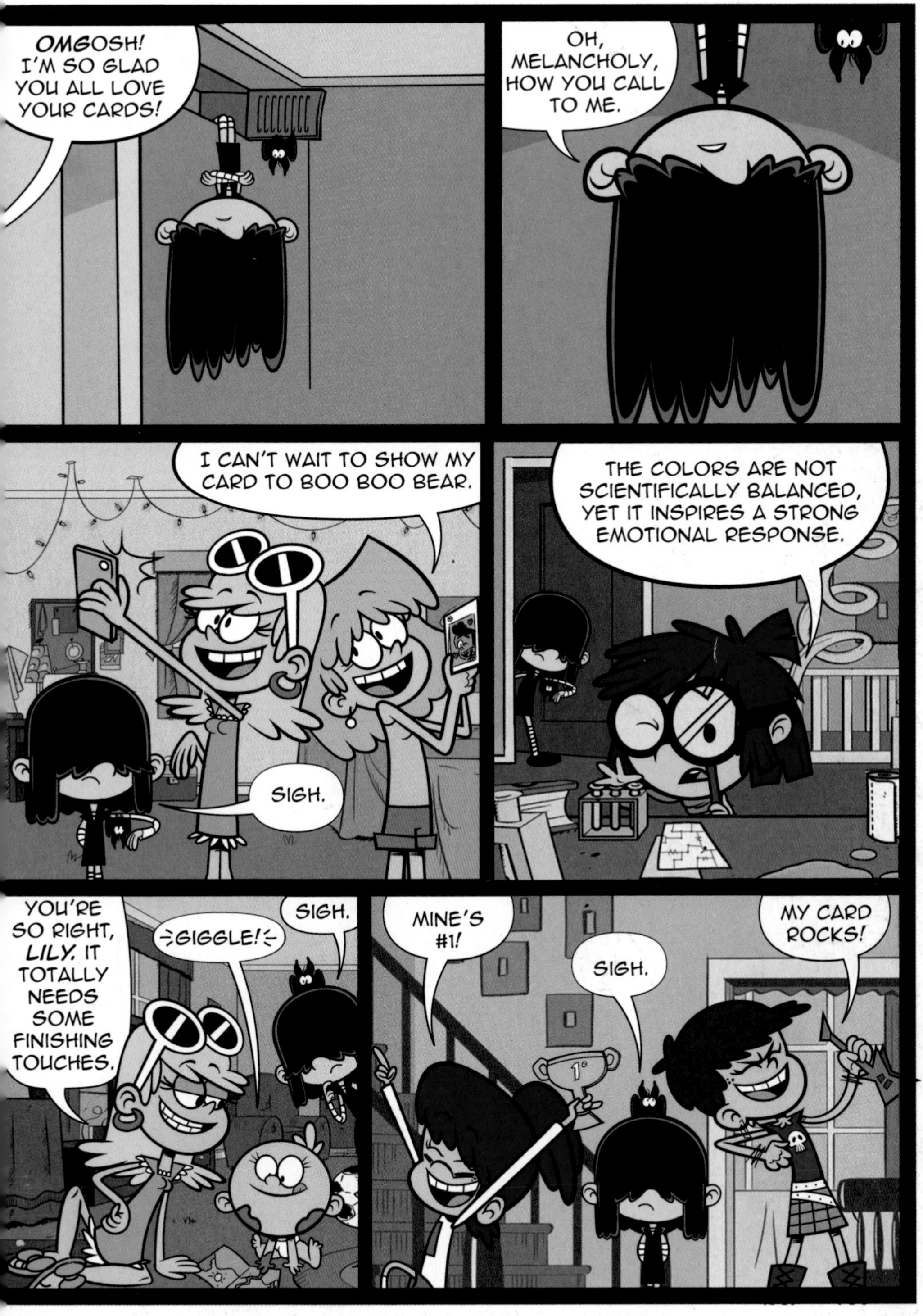
OMGOSH! I'M SO GLAD YOU ALL LOVE YOUR CARDS!
OH, MELANCHOLY, HOW YOU CALL TO ME.
I CAN'T WAIT TO SHOW MY CARD TO BOO BOO BEAR.
SIGH.
THE COLORS ARE NOT SCIENTIFICALLY BALANCED, YET IT INSPIRES A STRONG EMOTIONAL RESPONSE.
YOU'RE SO RIGHT, LILY. IT TOTALLY NEEDS SOME FINISHING TOUCHES.
GIGGLE!
SIGH.
MINE'S #1!
SIGH.
MY CARD ROCKS!

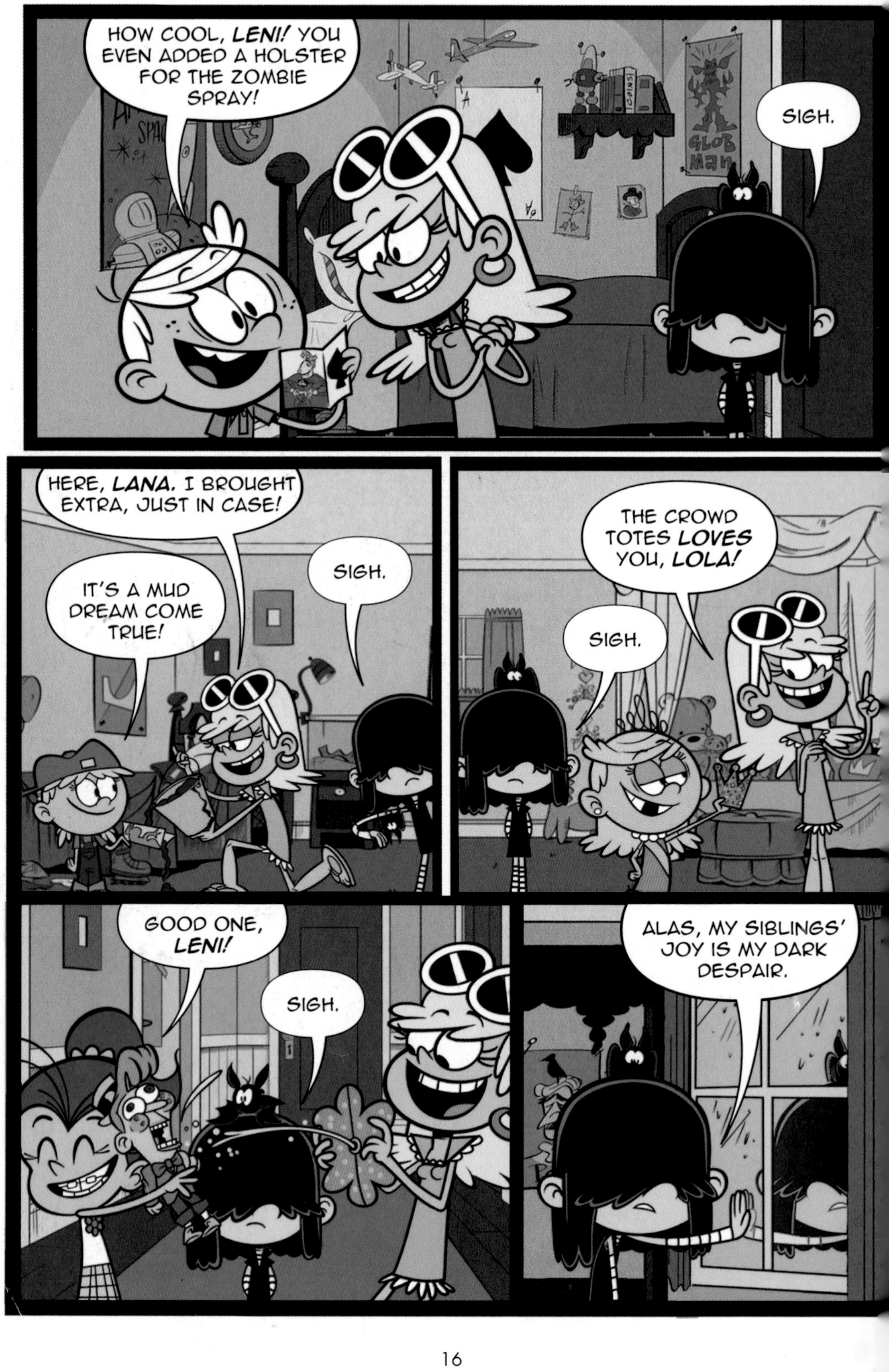
HOW COOL, **LENI!** YOU EVEN ADDED A HOLSTER FOR THE ZOMBIE SPRAY!
GLOB MAN
SIGH.
HERE, **LANA.** I BROUGHT EXTRA, JUST IN CASE!
IT'S A MUD DREAM COME TRUE!
SIGH.
THE CROWD TOTES **LOVES** YOU, **LOLA!**
SIGH.
GOOD ONE, **LENI!**
SIGH.
ALAS, MY SIBLINGS' JOY IS MY DARK DESPAIR.

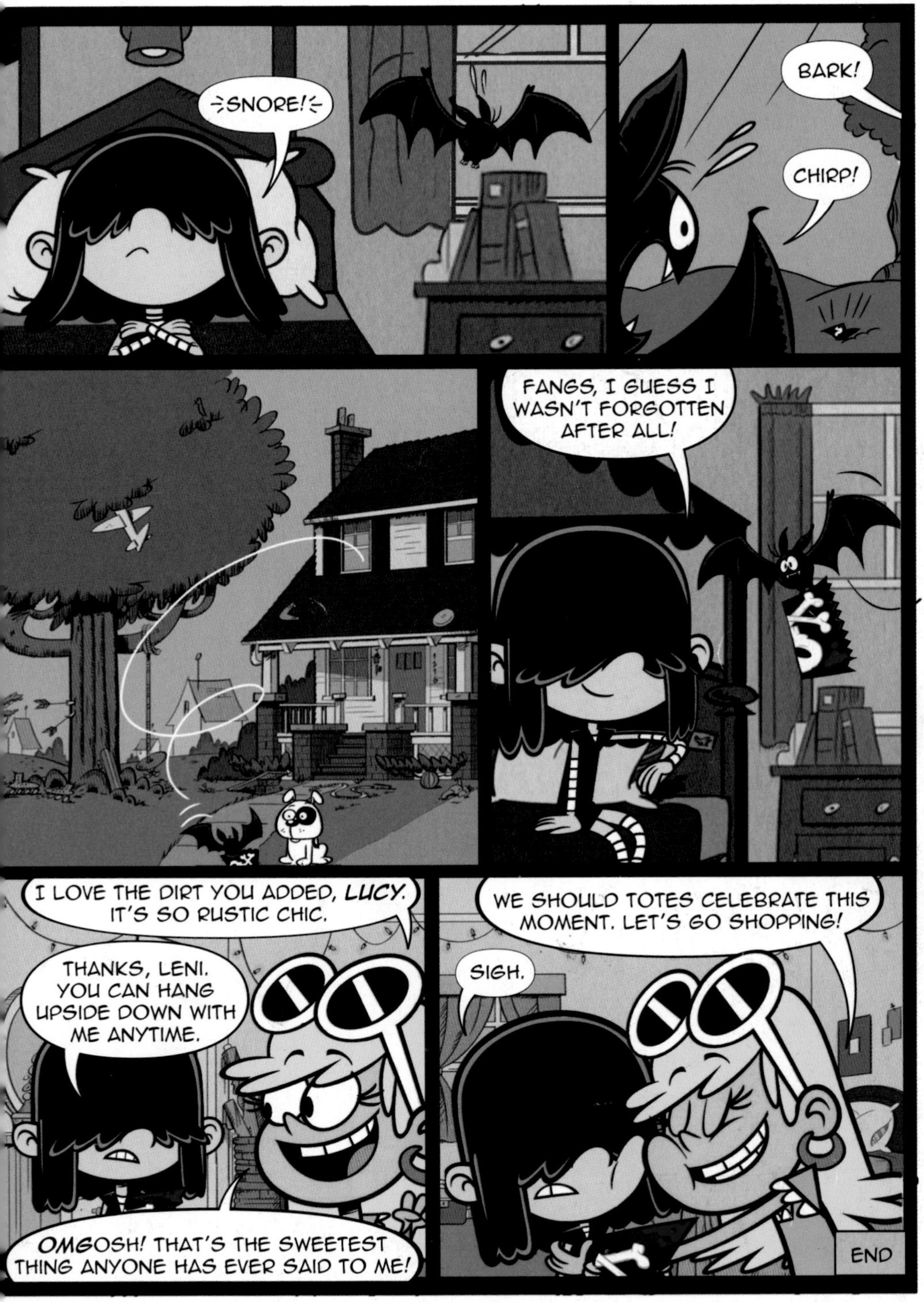

SNORE!
BARK!
CHIRP!
FANGS, I GUESS I WASN'T FORGOTTEN AFTER ALL!
I LOVE THE DIRT YOU ADDED, *LUCY*. IT'S SO RUSTIC CHIC.
THANKS, LENI. YOU CAN HANG UPSIDE DOWN WITH ME ANYTIME.
*OMG*OSH! THAT'S THE SWEETEST THING ANYONE HAS EVER SAID TO ME!
WE SHOULD TOTES CELEBRATE THIS MOMENT. LET'S GO SHOPPING!
SIGH.
END

"TWEETHEARTS"

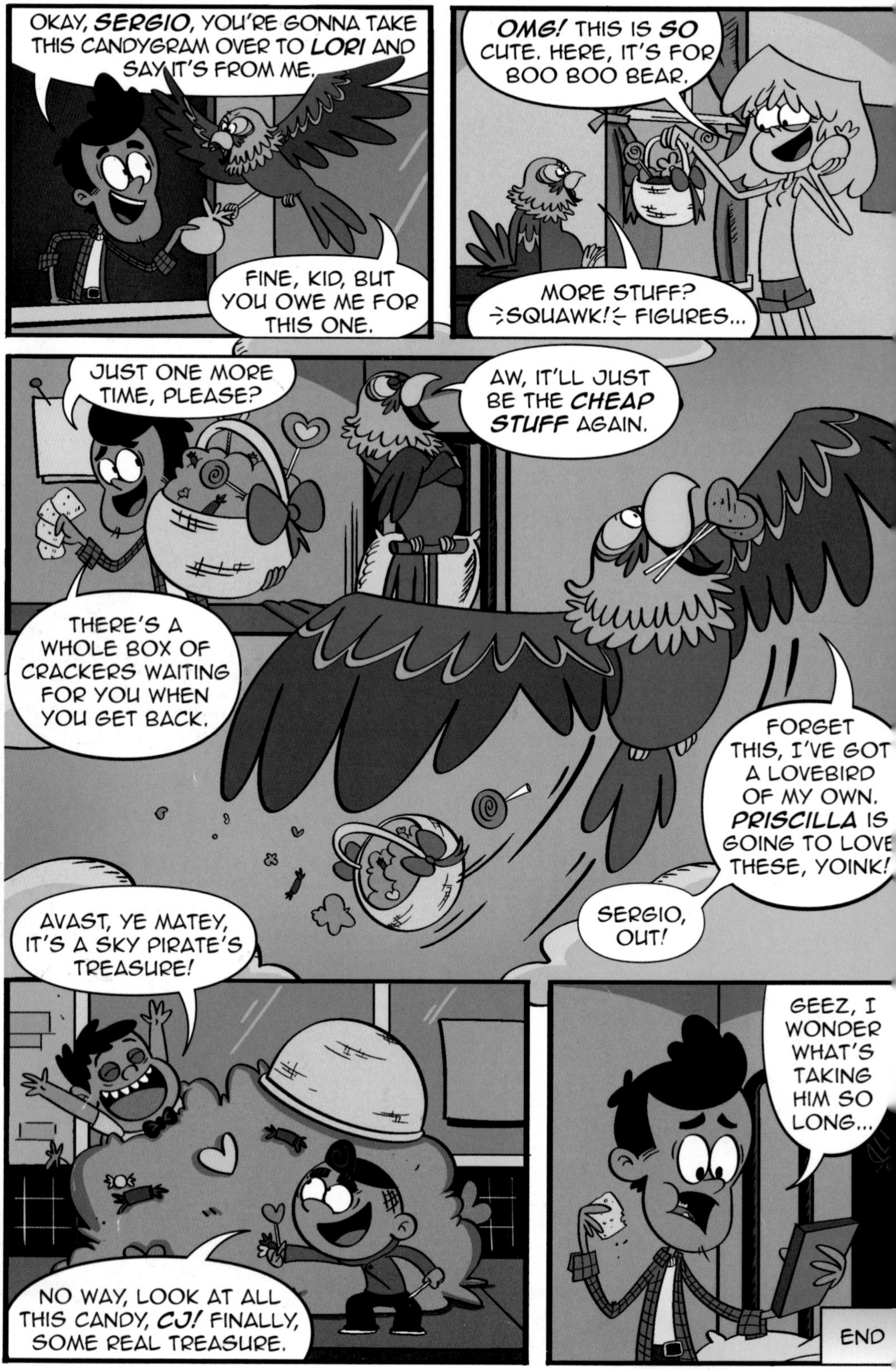

OKAY, SERGIO, YOU'RE GONNA TAKE THIS CANDYGRAM OVER TO LORI AND SAY IT'S FROM ME.
FINE, KID, BUT YOU OWE ME FOR THIS ONE.
OMG! THIS IS SO CUTE. HERE, IT'S FOR BOO BOO BEAR.
MORE STUFF? ⇉SQUAWK!⇇ FIGURES...
JUST ONE MORE TIME, PLEASE?
AW, IT'LL JUST BE THE CHEAP STUFF AGAIN.
THERE'S A WHOLE BOX OF CRACKERS WAITING FOR YOU WHEN YOU GET BACK.
FORGET THIS, I'VE GOT A LOVEBIRD OF MY OWN. PRISCILLA IS GOING TO LOVE THESE, YOINK!
SERGIO, OUT!
AVAST, YE MATEY, IT'S A SKY PIRATE'S TREASURE!
NO WAY, LOOK AT ALL THIS CANDY, CJ! FINALLY, SOME REAL TREASURE.
GEEZ, I WONDER WHAT'S TAKING HIM SO LONG...
END

"WHAT'S LOVE GOT TO DO WITH IT?"

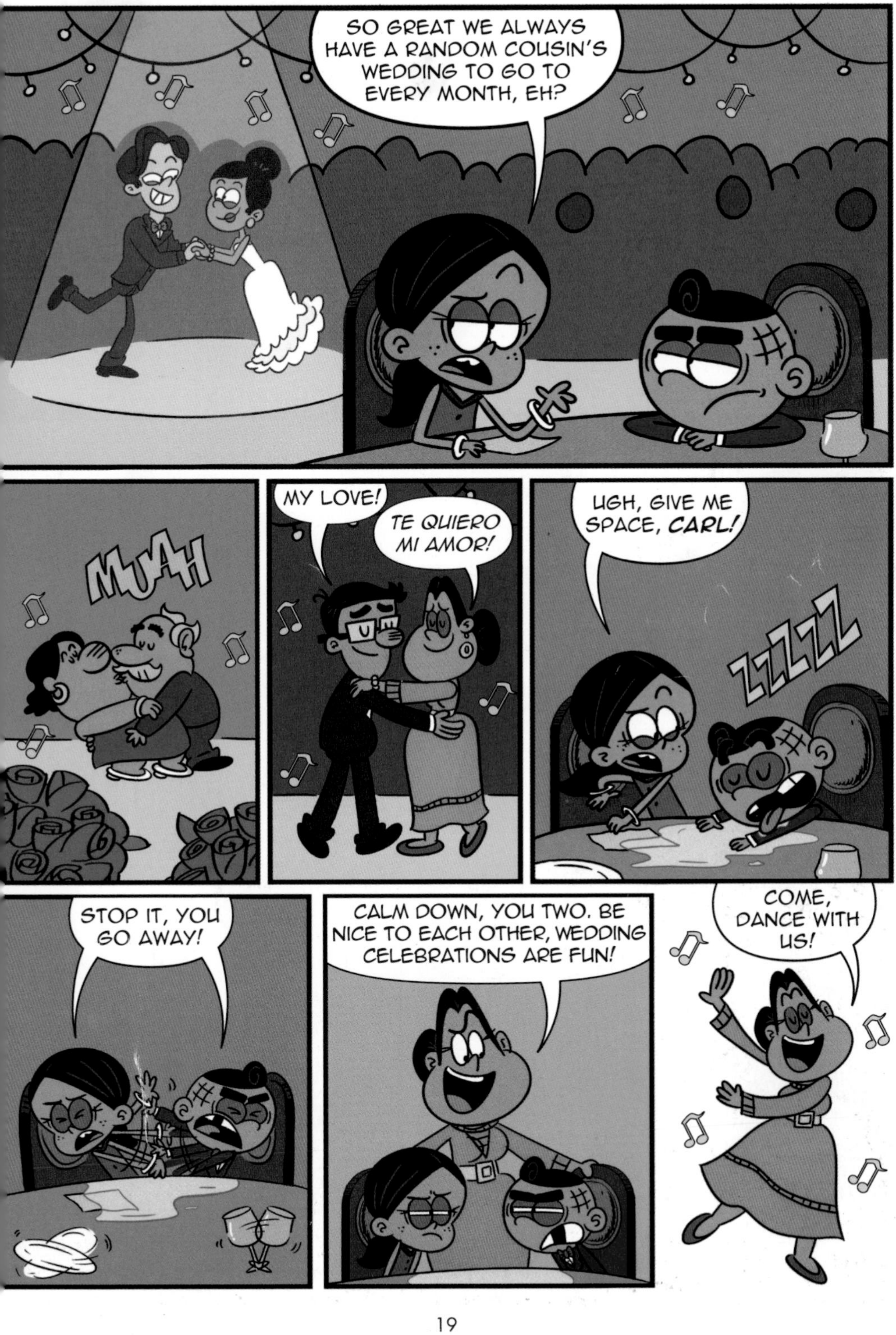

SO GREAT WE ALWAYS HAVE A RANDOM COUSIN'S WEDDING TO GO TO EVERY MONTH, EH?
MUAH
MY LOVE!
TE QUIERO MI AMOR!
UGH, GIVE ME SPACE, CARL!
ZZZZZ
STOP IT, YOU GO AWAY!
CALM DOWN, YOU TWO. BE NICE TO EACH OTHER, WEDDING CELEBRATIONS ARE FUN!
COME, DANCE WITH US!

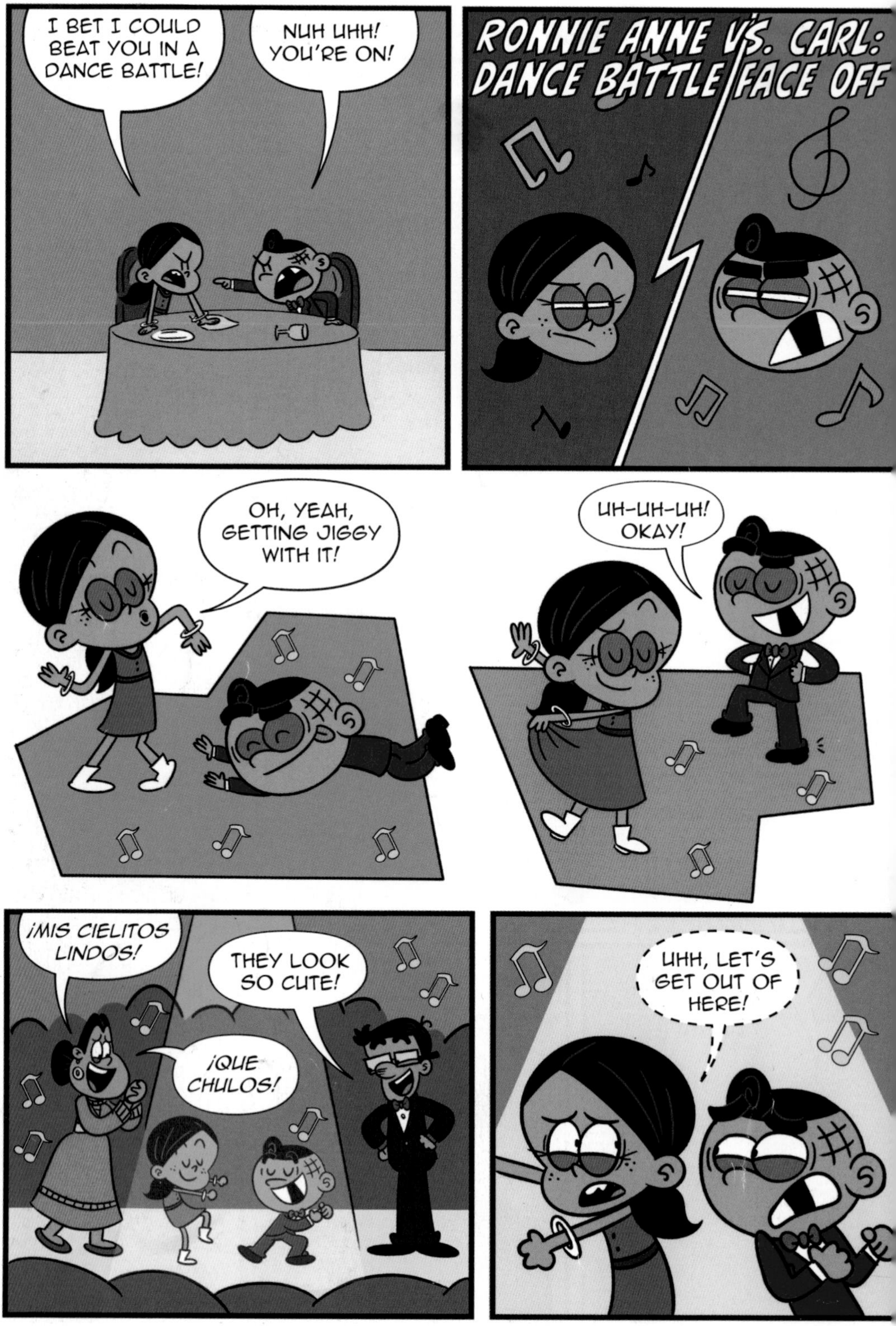
I BET I COULD BEAT YOU IN A DANCE BATTLE!
NUH UHH! YOU'RE ON!
RONNIE ANNE VS. CARL: DANCE BATTLE FACE OFF
OH, YEAH, GETTING JIGGY WITH IT!
UH-UH-UH! OKAY!
¡MIS CIELITOS LINDOS!
THEY LOOK SO CUTE!
¡QUE CHULOS!
UHH, LET'S GET OUT OF HERE!

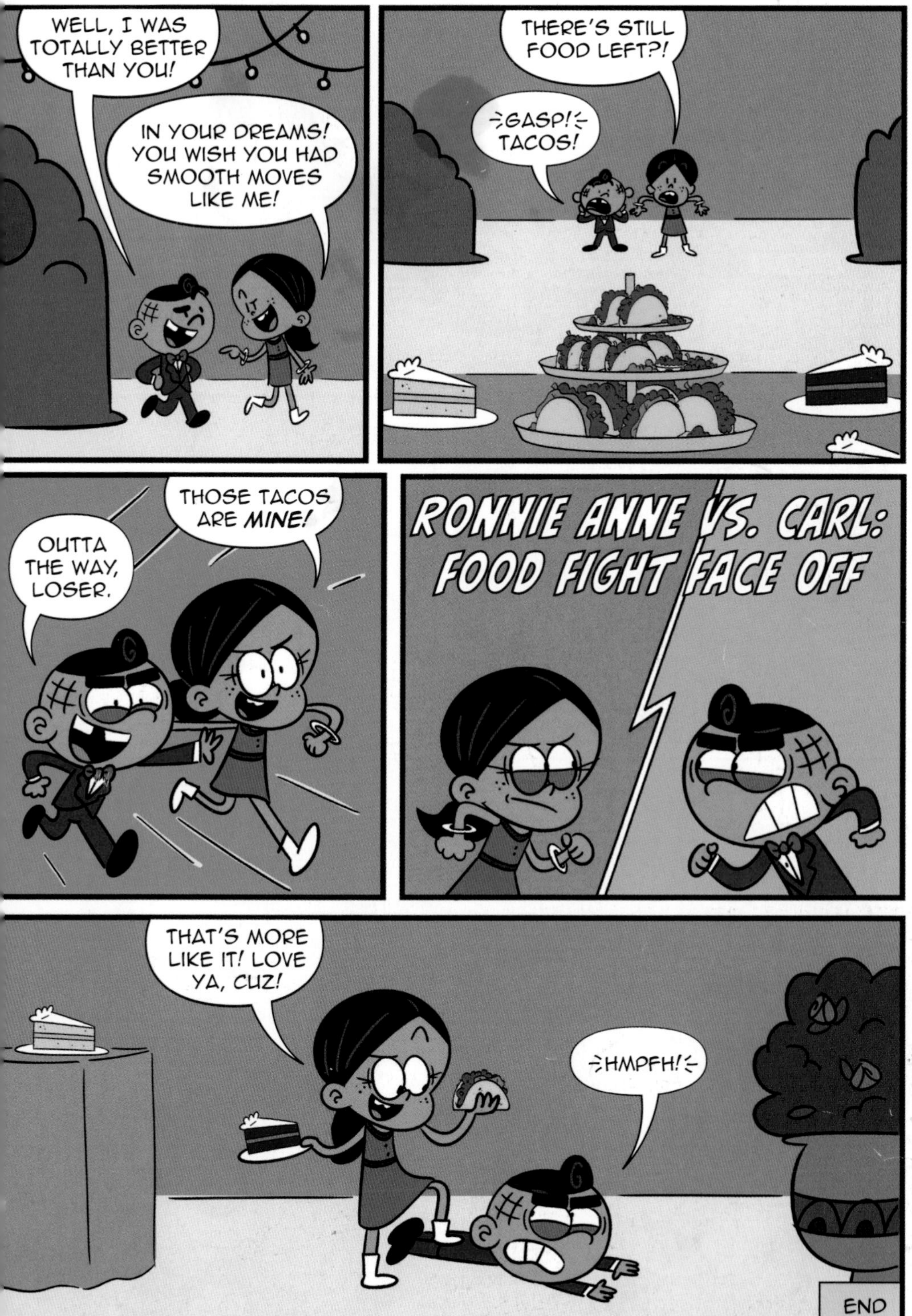
WELL, I WAS TOTALLY BETTER THAN YOU!
IN YOUR DREAMS! YOU WISH YOU HAD SMOOTH MOVES LIKE ME!
THERE'S STILL FOOD LEFT?!
GASP! TACOS!
THOSE TACOS ARE MINE!
OUTTA THE WAY, LOSER.
RONNIE ANNE VS. CARL: FOOD FIGHT FACE OFF
THAT'S MORE LIKE IT! LOVE YA, CUZ!
HMPFH!
END

"CUPID'S WINGS"

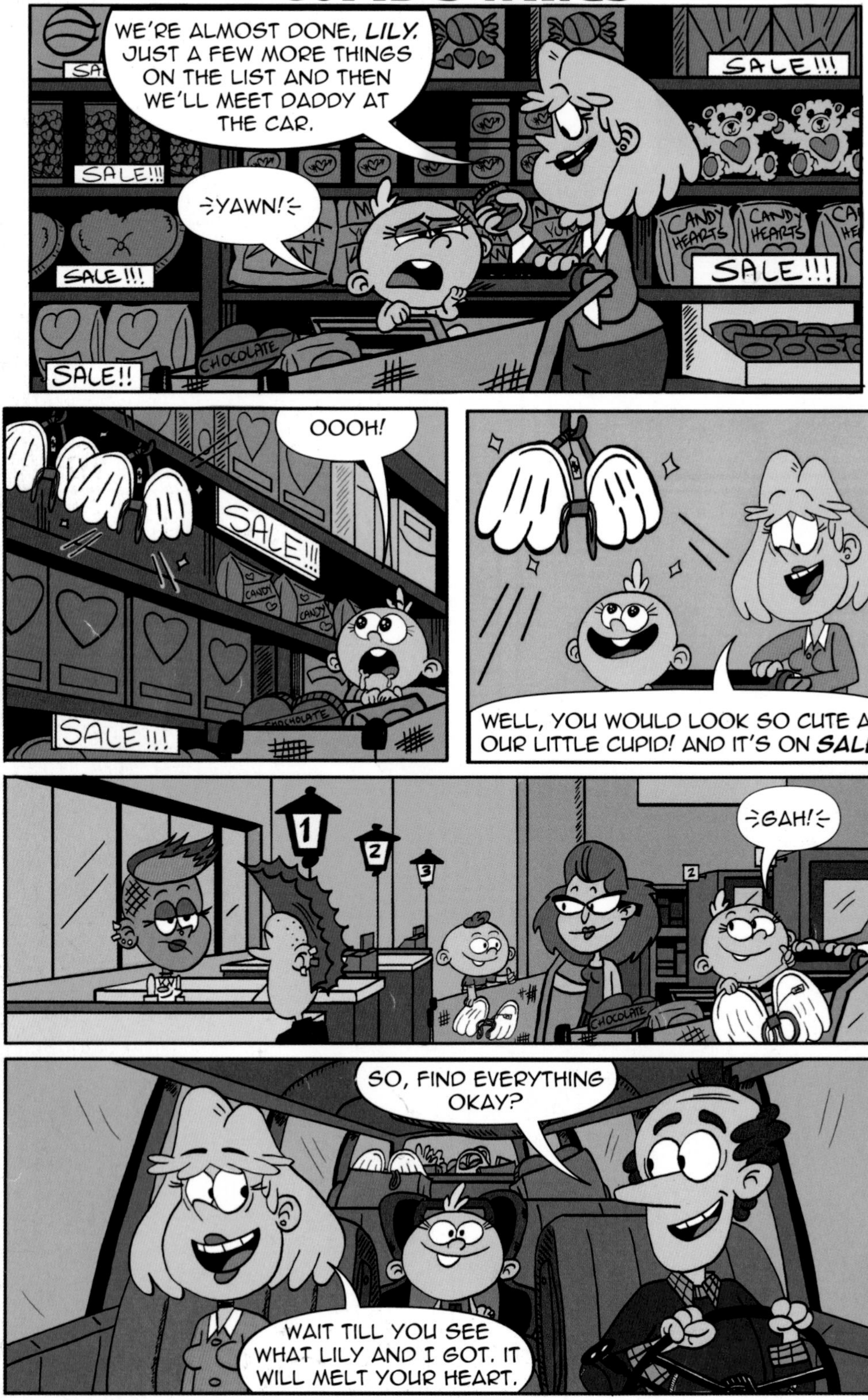

WE'RE ALMOST DONE, LILY. JUST A FEW MORE THINGS ON THE LIST AND THEN WE'LL MEET DADDY AT THE CAR.
YAWN!
SALE!!!
CANDY HEARTS
CHOCOLATE
OOOH!
SALE!!!
WELL, YOU WOULD LOOK SO CUTE AS OUR LITTLE CUPID! AND IT'S ON SALE.
GAH!
SO, FIND EVERYTHING OKAY?
WAIT TILL YOU SEE WHAT LILY AND I GOT. IT WILL MELT YOUR HEART.

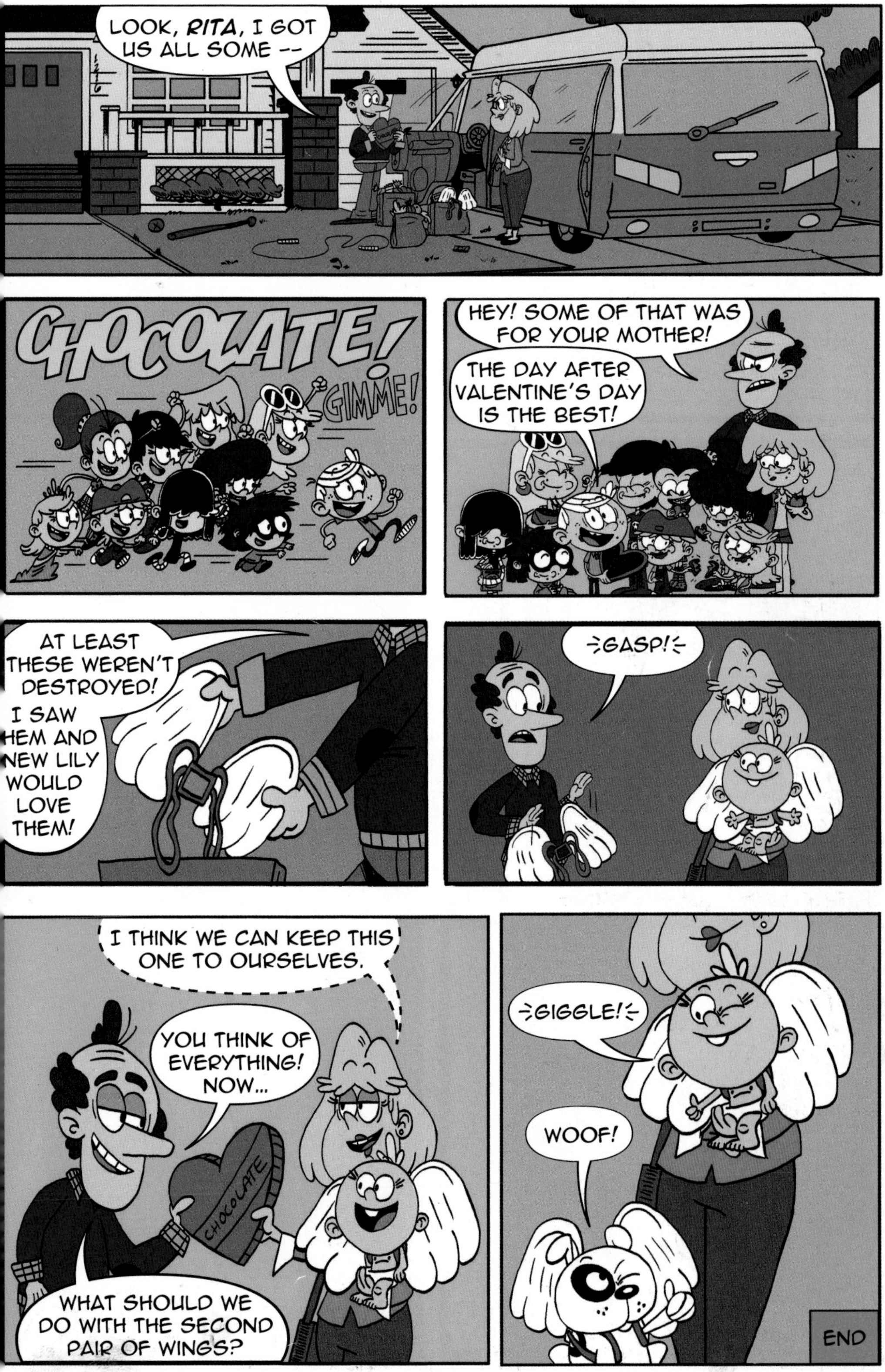
LOOK, RITA, I GOT US ALL SOME --
CHOCOLATE!
GIMME!
HEY! SOME OF THAT WAS FOR YOUR MOTHER!
THE DAY AFTER VALENTINE'S DAY IS THE BEST!
AT LEAST THESE WEREN'T DESTROYED!
I SAW HEM AND NEW LILY WOULD LOVE THEM!
GASP!
I THINK WE CAN KEEP THIS ONE TO OURSELVES.
YOU THINK OF EVERYTHING! NOW...
CHOCOLATE
WHAT SHOULD WE DO WITH THE SECOND PAIR OF WINGS?
GIGGLE!
WOOF!
END

"FOR THE LOVE OF THE GAME"

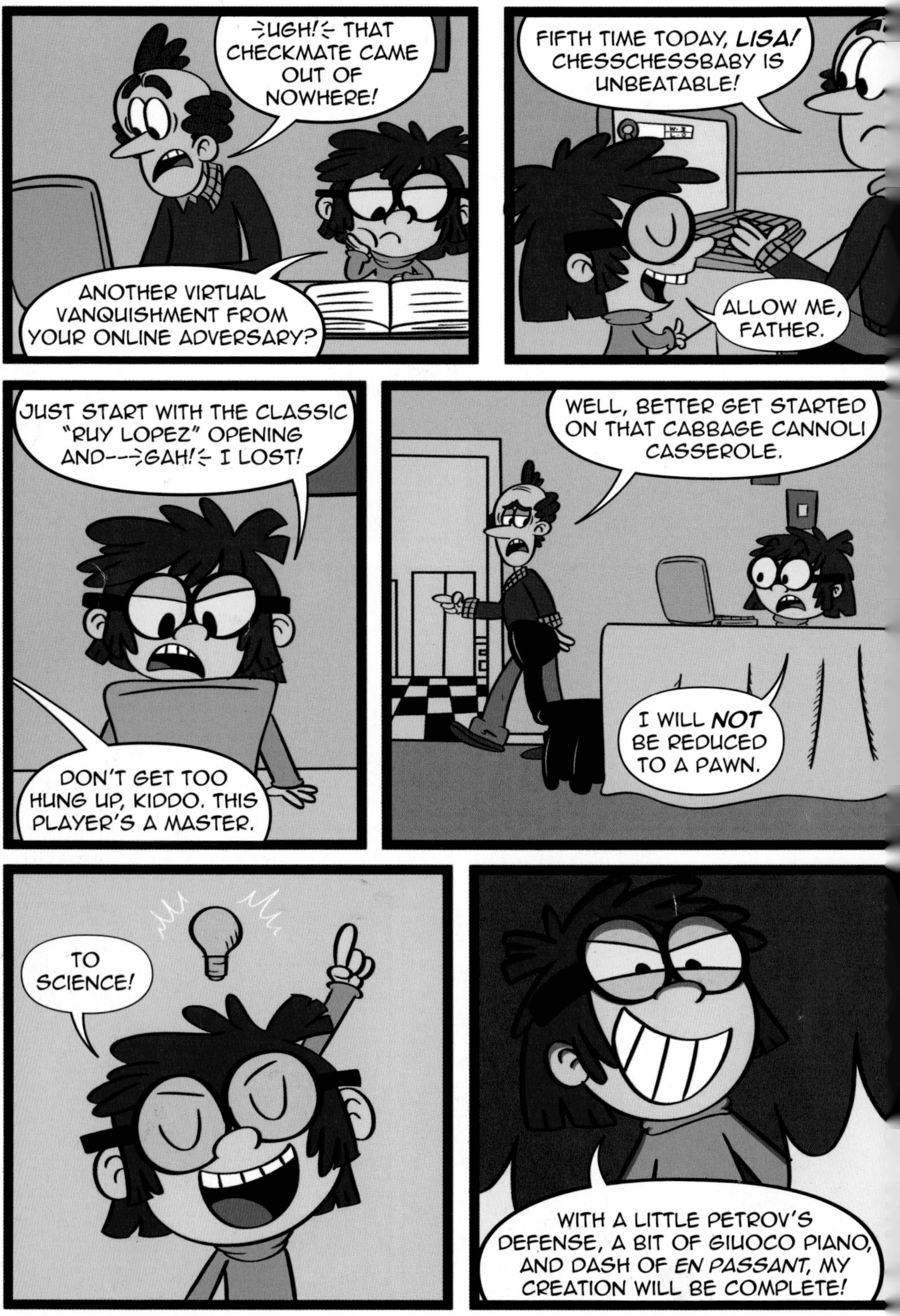
UGH! THAT CHECKMATE CAME OUT OF NOWHERE!
ANOTHER VIRTUAL VANQUISHMENT FROM YOUR ONLINE ADVERSARY?
FIFTH TIME TODAY, LISA! CHESSCHESSBABY IS UNBEATABLE!
ALLOW ME, FATHER.
JUST START WITH THE CLASSIC "RUY LOPEZ" OPENING AND--GAH! I LOST!
DON'T GET TOO HUNG UP, KIDDO. THIS PLAYER'S A MASTER.
WELL, BETTER GET STARTED ON THAT CABBAGE CANNOLI CASSEROLE.
I WILL NOT BE REDUCED TO A PAWN.
TO SCIENCE!
WITH A LITTLE PETROV'S DEFENSE, A BIT OF GIUOCO PIANO, AND DASH OF EN PASSANT, MY CREATION WILL BE COMPLETE!

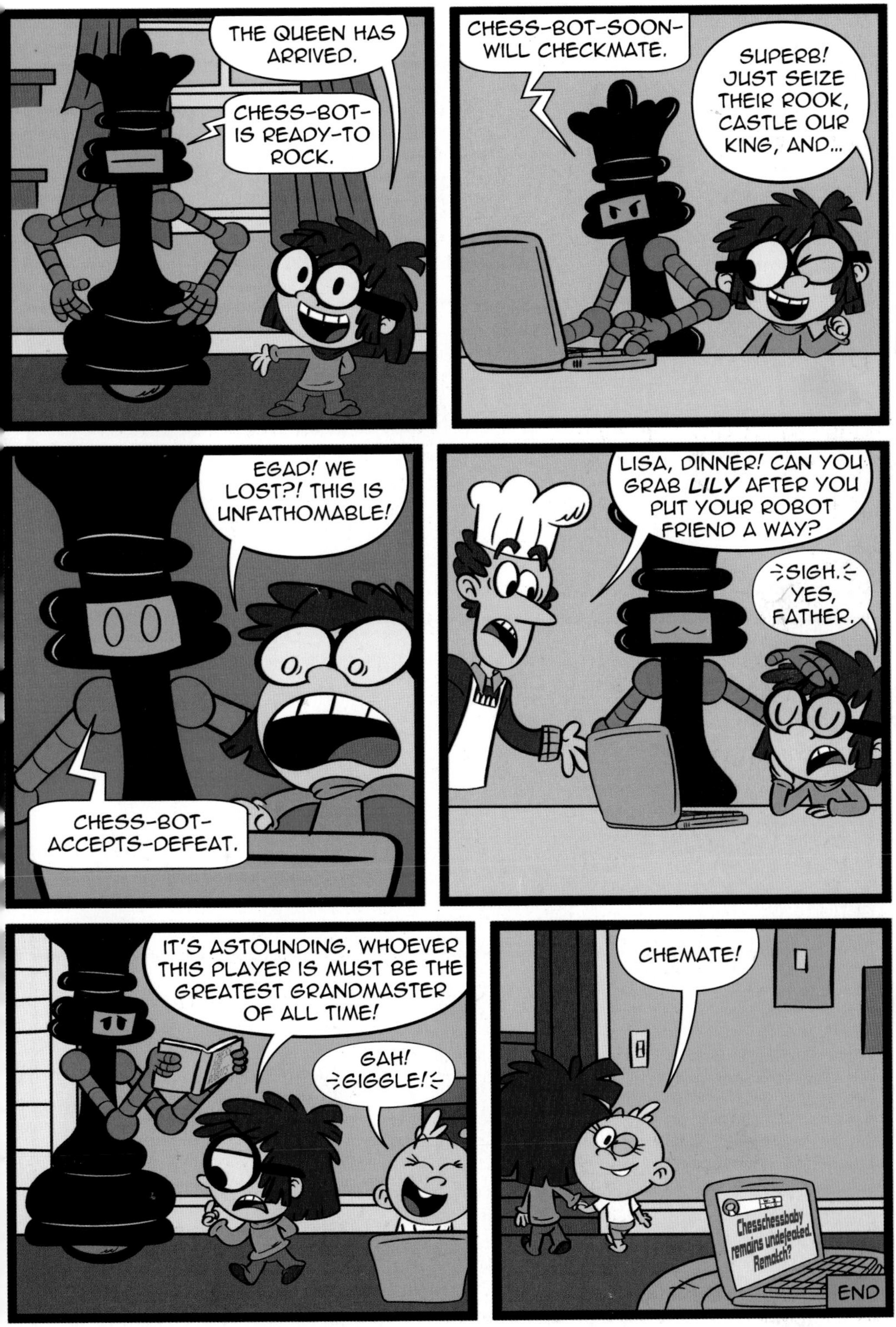
THE QUEEN HAS ARRIVED.
CHESS-BOT-IS READY-TO ROCK.
CHESS-BOT-SOON-WILL CHECKMATE.
SUPERB! JUST SEIZE THEIR ROOK, CASTLE OUR KING, AND...
EGAD! WE LOST?! THIS IS UNFATHOMABLE!
CHESS-BOT-ACCEPTS-DEFEAT.
LISA, DINNER! CAN YOU GRAB LILY AFTER YOU PUT YOUR ROBOT FRIEND A WAY?
SIGH. YES, FATHER.
IT'S ASTOUNDING. WHOEVER THIS PLAYER IS MUST BE THE GREATEST GRANDMASTER OF ALL TIME!
GAH! GIGGLE!
CHEMATE!
Chesschessbaby remains undefeated. Rematch?
END

"OVER THE LINE"

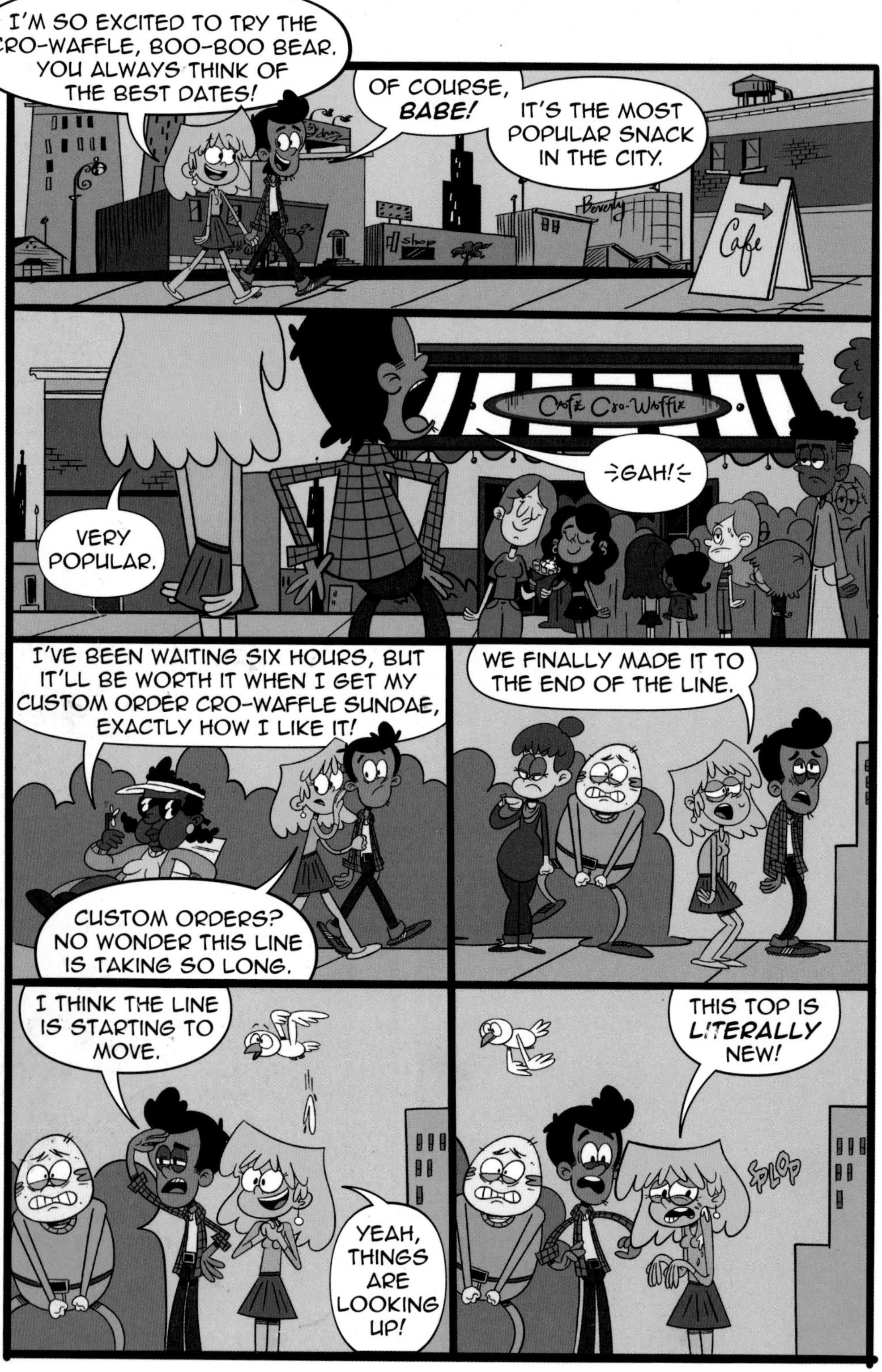
I'M SO EXCITED TO TRY THE CRO-WAFFLE, BOO-BOO BEAR. YOU ALWAYS THINK OF THE BEST DATES!
OF COURSE, BABE!
IT'S THE MOST POPULAR SNACK IN THE CITY.
Beverly
Cafe
CAFÉ CRO-WAFFLE
GAH!
VERY POPULAR.
I'VE BEEN WAITING SIX HOURS, BUT IT'LL BE WORTH IT WHEN I GET MY CUSTOM ORDER CRO-WAFFLE SUNDAE, EXACTLY HOW I LIKE IT!
CUSTOM ORDERS? NO WONDER THIS LINE IS TAKING SO LONG.
WE FINALLY MADE IT TO THE END OF THE LINE.
I THINK THE LINE IS STARTING TO MOVE.
YEAH, THINGS ARE LOOKING UP!
THIS TOP IS LITERALLY NEW!
SPLOP

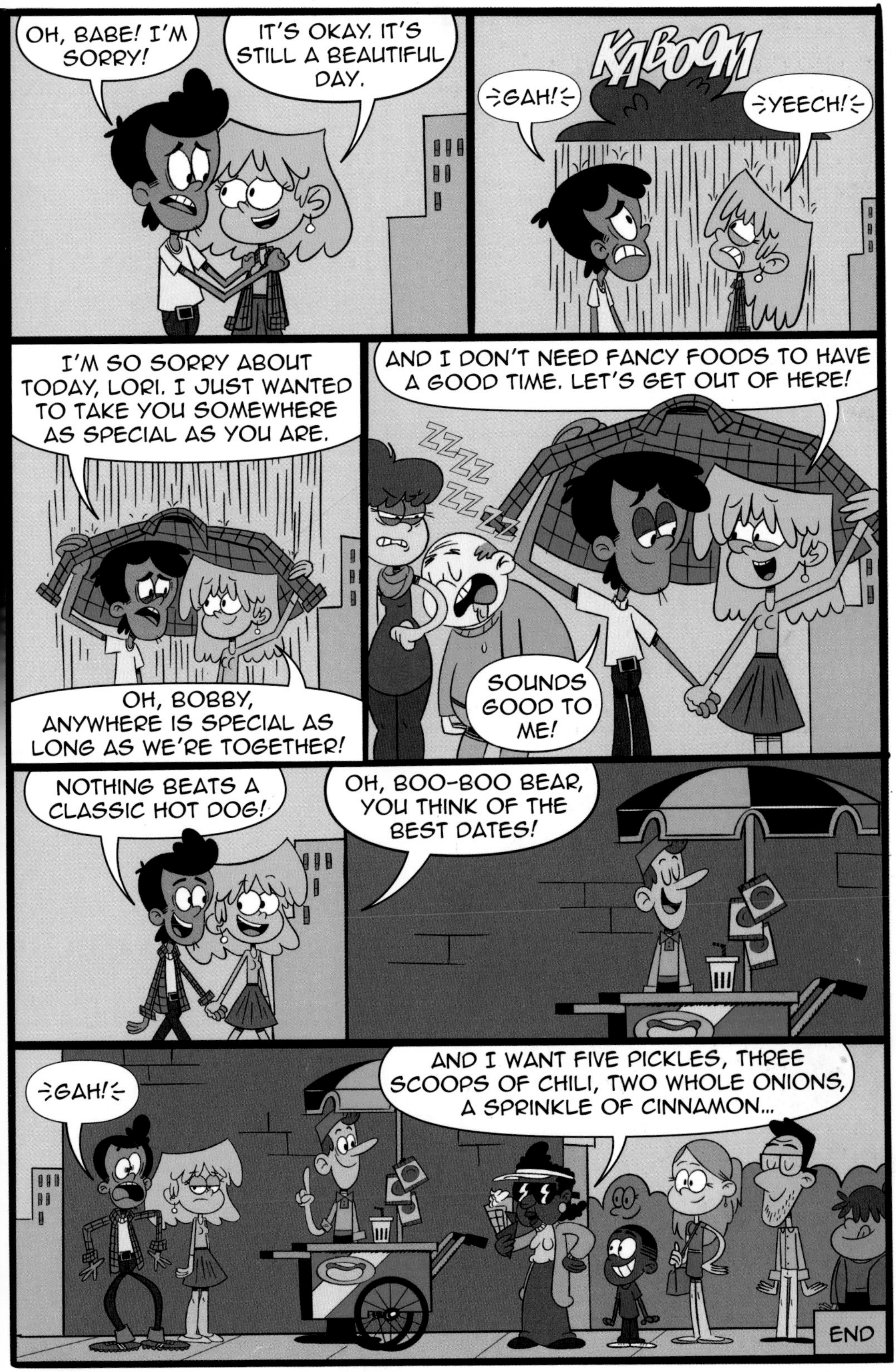
OH, BABE! I'M SORRY!
IT'S OKAY. IT'S STILL A BEAUTIFUL DAY.
KABOOM
GAH!
YEECH!
I'M SO SORRY ABOUT TODAY, LORI. I JUST WANTED TO TAKE YOU SOMEWHERE AS SPECIAL AS YOU ARE.
OH, BOBBY, ANYWHERE IS SPECIAL AS LONG AS WE'RE TOGETHER!
AND I DON'T NEED FANCY FOODS TO HAVE A GOOD TIME. LET'S GET OUT OF HERE!
ZZZZ ZZZZ
SOUNDS GOOD TO ME!
NOTHING BEATS A CLASSIC HOT DOG!
OH, BOO-BOO BEAR, YOU THINK OF THE BEST DATES!
GAH!
AND I WANT FIVE PICKLES, THREE SCOOPS OF CHILI, TWO WHOLE ONIONS, A SPRINKLE OF CINNAMON...
END

"MADE WITH CARE"

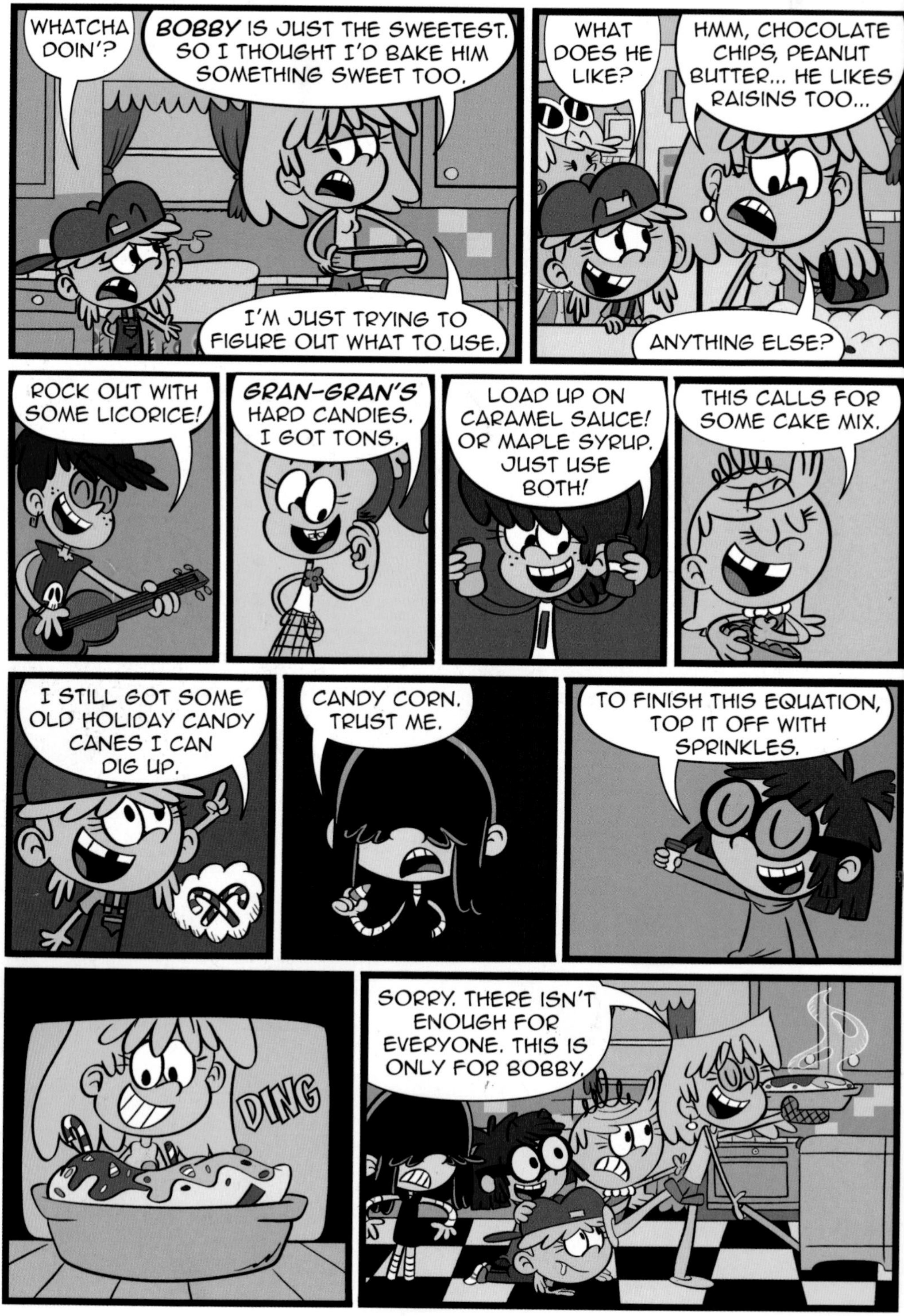
WHATCHA DOIN'?
BOBBY IS JUST THE SWEETEST. SO I THOUGHT I'D BAKE HIM SOMETHING SWEET TOO.
I'M JUST TRYING TO FIGURE OUT WHAT TO USE.
WHAT DOES HE LIKE?
HMM, CHOCOLATE CHIPS, PEANUT BUTTER... HE LIKES RAISINS TOO...
ANYTHING ELSE?
ROCK OUT WITH SOME LICORICE!
GRAN-GRAN'S HARD CANDIES. I GOT TONS.
LOAD UP ON CARAMEL SAUCE! OR MAPLE SYRUP. JUST USE BOTH!
THIS CALLS FOR SOME CAKE MIX.
I STILL GOT SOME OLD HOLIDAY CANDY CANES I CAN DIG UP.
CANDY CORN. TRUST ME.
TO FINISH THIS EQUATION, TOP IT OFF WITH SPRINKLES.
DING
SORRY. THERE ISN'T ENOUGH FOR EVERYONE. THIS IS ONLY FOR BOBBY.

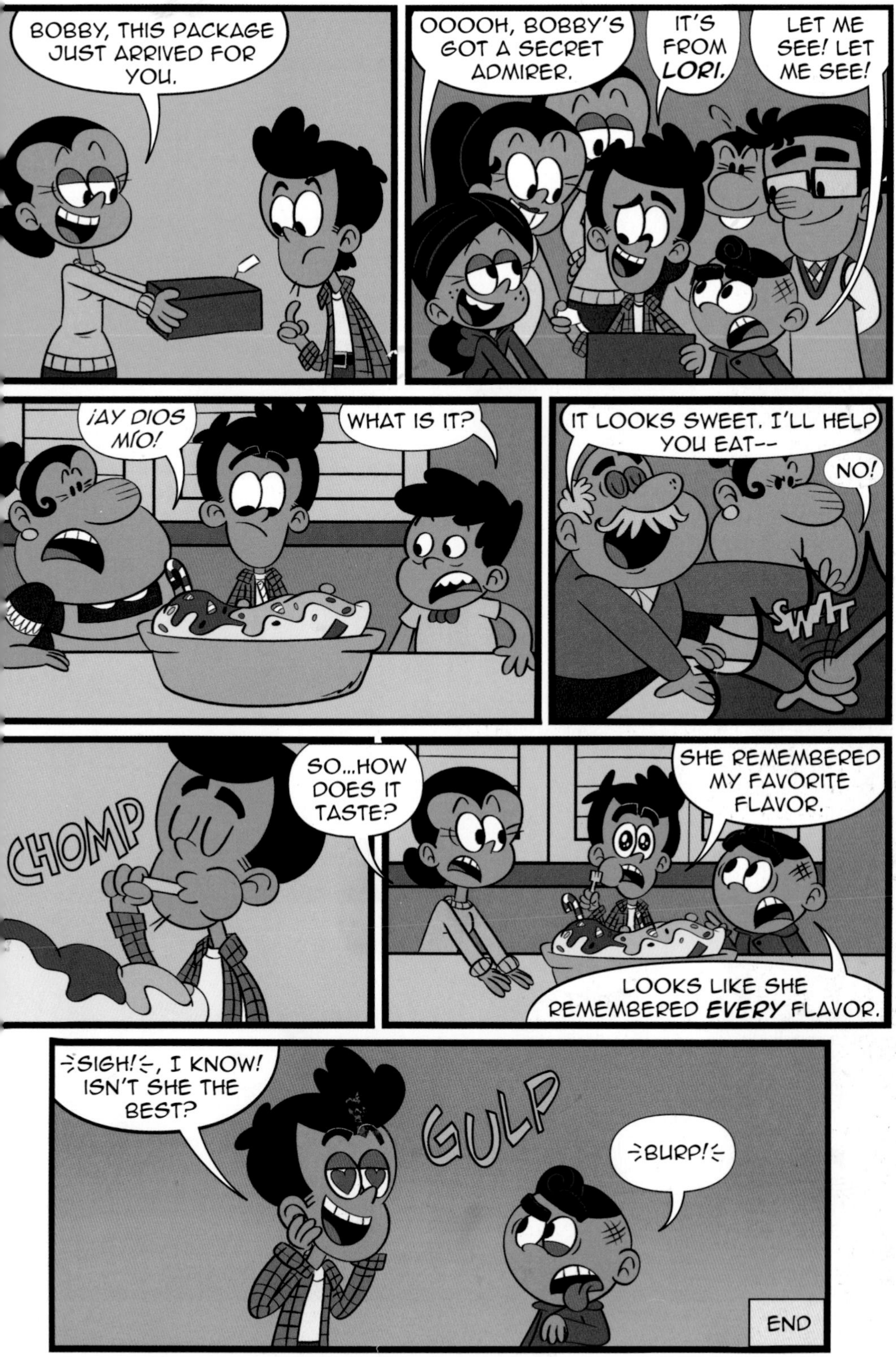
BOBBY, THIS PACKAGE JUST ARRIVED FOR YOU.
OOOOH, BOBBY'S GOT A SECRET ADMIRER.
IT'S FROM LORI.
LET ME SEE! LET ME SEE!
¡AY DIOS MÍO!
WHAT IS IT?
IT LOOKS SWEET. I'LL HELP YOU EAT--
NO!
SWAT
CHOMP
SO...HOW DOES IT TASTE?
SHE REMEMBERED MY FAVORITE FLAVOR.
LOOKS LIKE SHE REMEMBERED EVERY FLAVOR.
SIGH!, I KNOW! ISN'T SHE THE BEST?
GULP
BURP!
END

"SENIOR PROM"

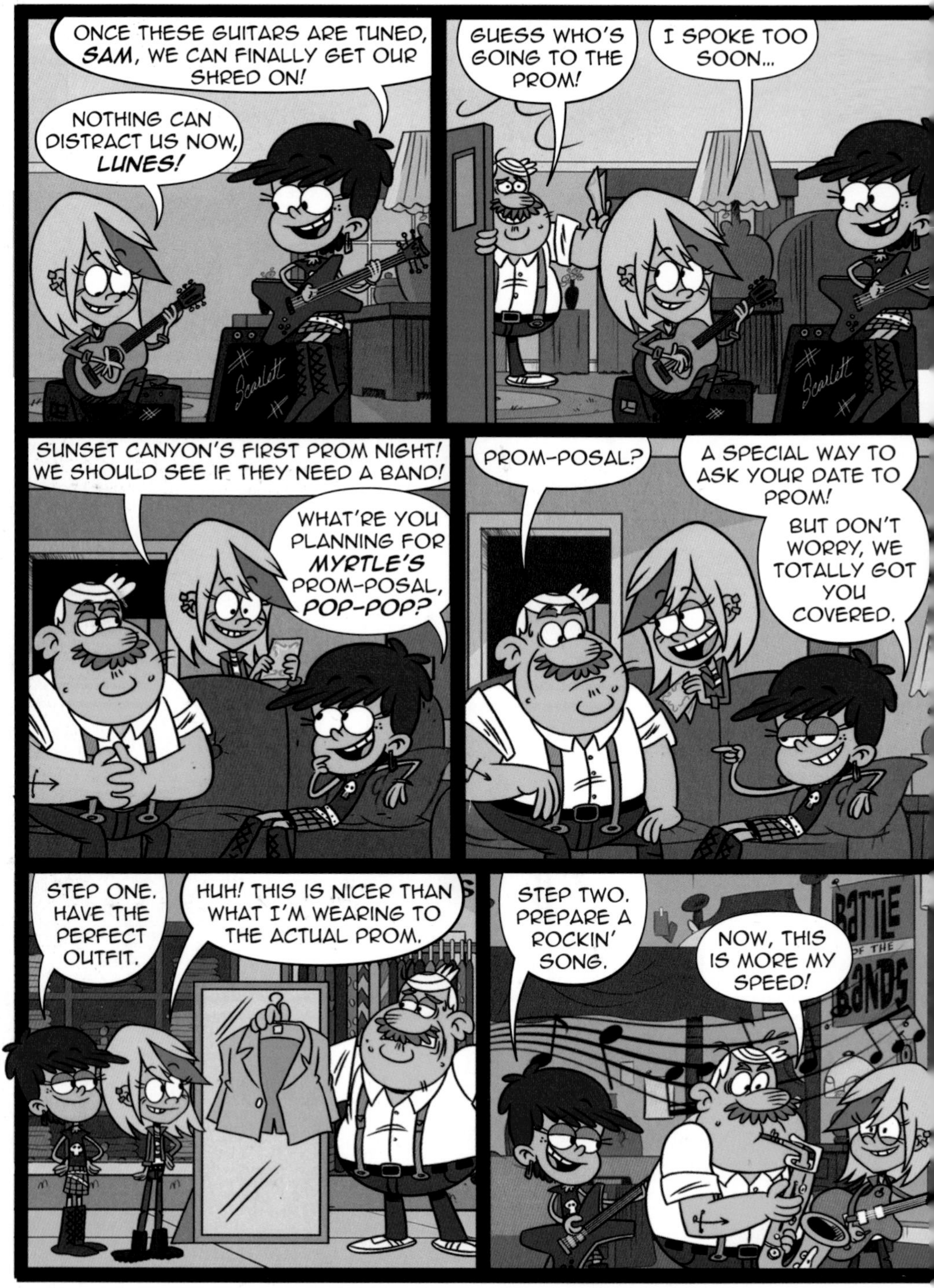

ONCE THESE GUITARS ARE TUNED, SAM, WE CAN FINALLY GET OUR SHRED ON!
NOTHING CAN DISTRACT US NOW, LUNES!
Scarlett
GUESS WHO'S GOING TO THE PROM!
I SPOKE TOO SOON...
Scarlett
SUNSET CANYON'S FIRST PROM NIGHT! WE SHOULD SEE IF THEY NEED A BAND!
WHAT'RE YOU PLANNING FOR MYRTLE'S PROM-POSAL, POP-POP?
PROM-POSAL?
A SPECIAL WAY TO ASK YOUR DATE TO PROM!
BUT DON'T WORRY, WE TOTALLY GOT YOU COVERED.
STEP ONE. HAVE THE PERFECT OUTFIT.
HUH! THIS IS NICER THAN WHAT I'M WEARING TO THE ACTUAL PROM.
STEP TWO. PREPARE A ROCKIN' SONG.
NOW, THIS IS MORE MY SPEED!
BATTLE OF THE BANDS

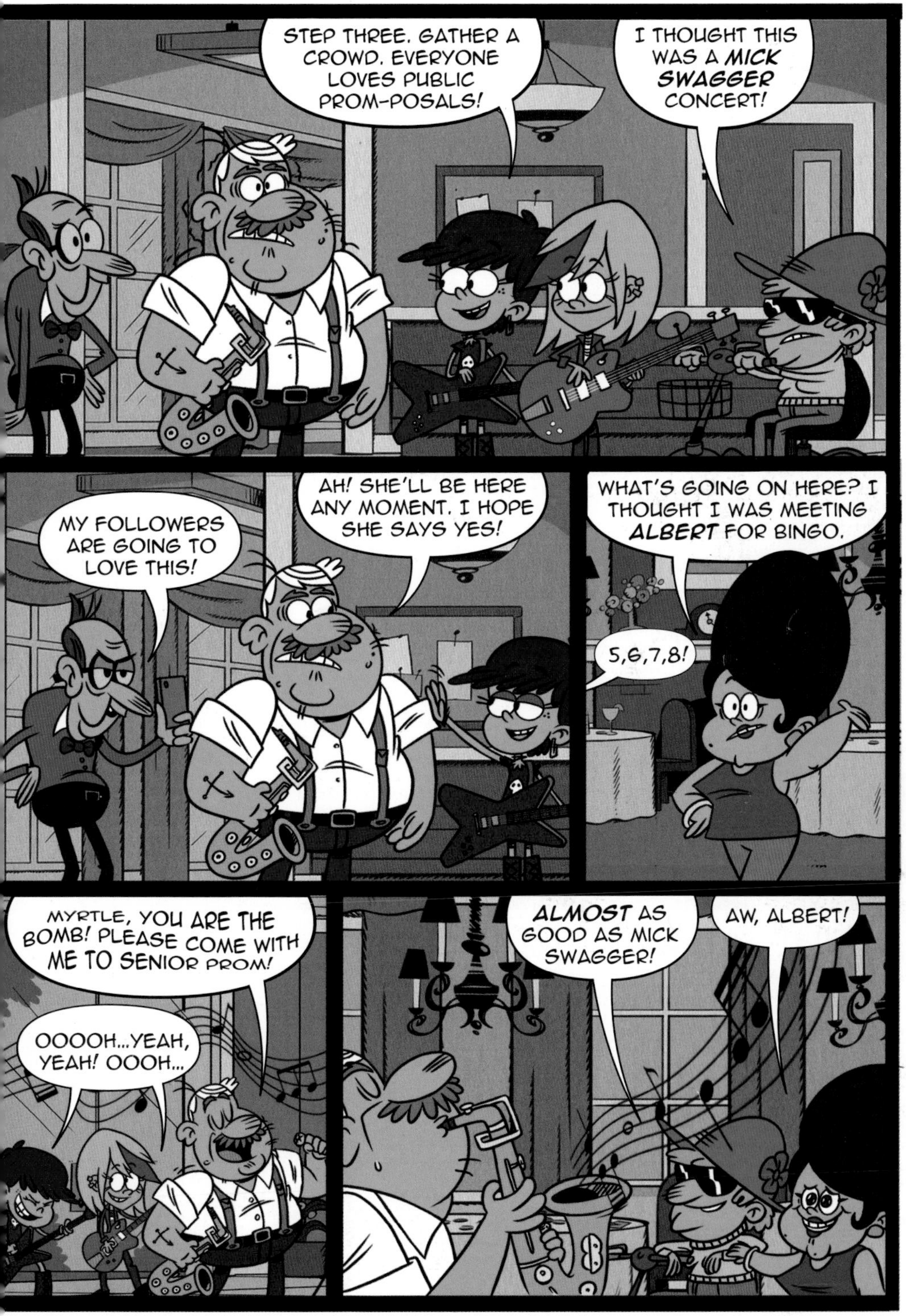
STEP THREE. GATHER A CROWD. EVERYONE LOVES PUBLIC PROM-POSALS!
I THOUGHT THIS WAS A MICK SWAGGER CONCERT!
MY FOLLOWERS ARE GOING TO LOVE THIS!
AH! SHE'LL BE HERE ANY MOMENT. I HOPE SHE SAYS YES!
WHAT'S GOING ON HERE? I THOUGHT I WAS MEETING ALBERT FOR BINGO.
5,6,7,8!
MYRTLE, YOU ARE THE BOMB! PLEASE COME WITH ME TO SENIOR PROM!
OOOOH...YEAH, YEAH! OOOH...
ALMOST AS GOOD AS MICK SWAGGER!
AW, ALBERT!

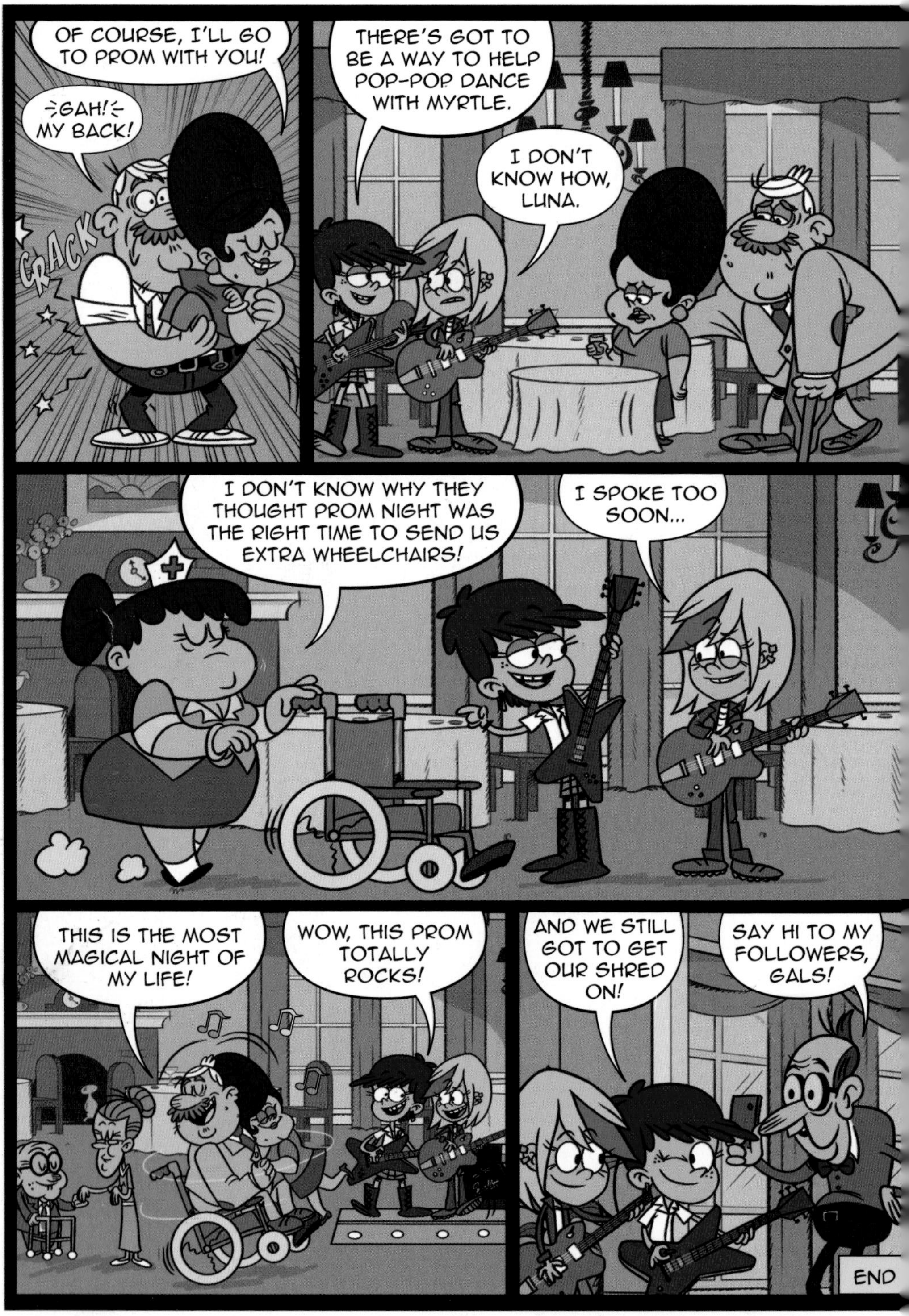
OF COURSE, I'LL GO TO PROM WITH YOU!
GAH! MY BACK!
CRACK
THERE'S GOT TO BE A WAY TO HELP POP-POP DANCE WITH MYRTLE.
I DON'T KNOW HOW, LUNA.
I DON'T KNOW WHY THEY THOUGHT PROM NIGHT WAS THE RIGHT TIME TO SEND US EXTRA WHEELCHAIRS!
I SPOKE TOO SOON...
THIS IS THE MOST MAGICAL NIGHT OF MY LIFE!
WOW, THIS PROM TOTALLY ROCKS!
AND WE STILL GOT TO GET OUR SHRED ON!
SAY HI TO MY FOLLOWERS, GALS!
END

“O-PUN-ING NIGHT”

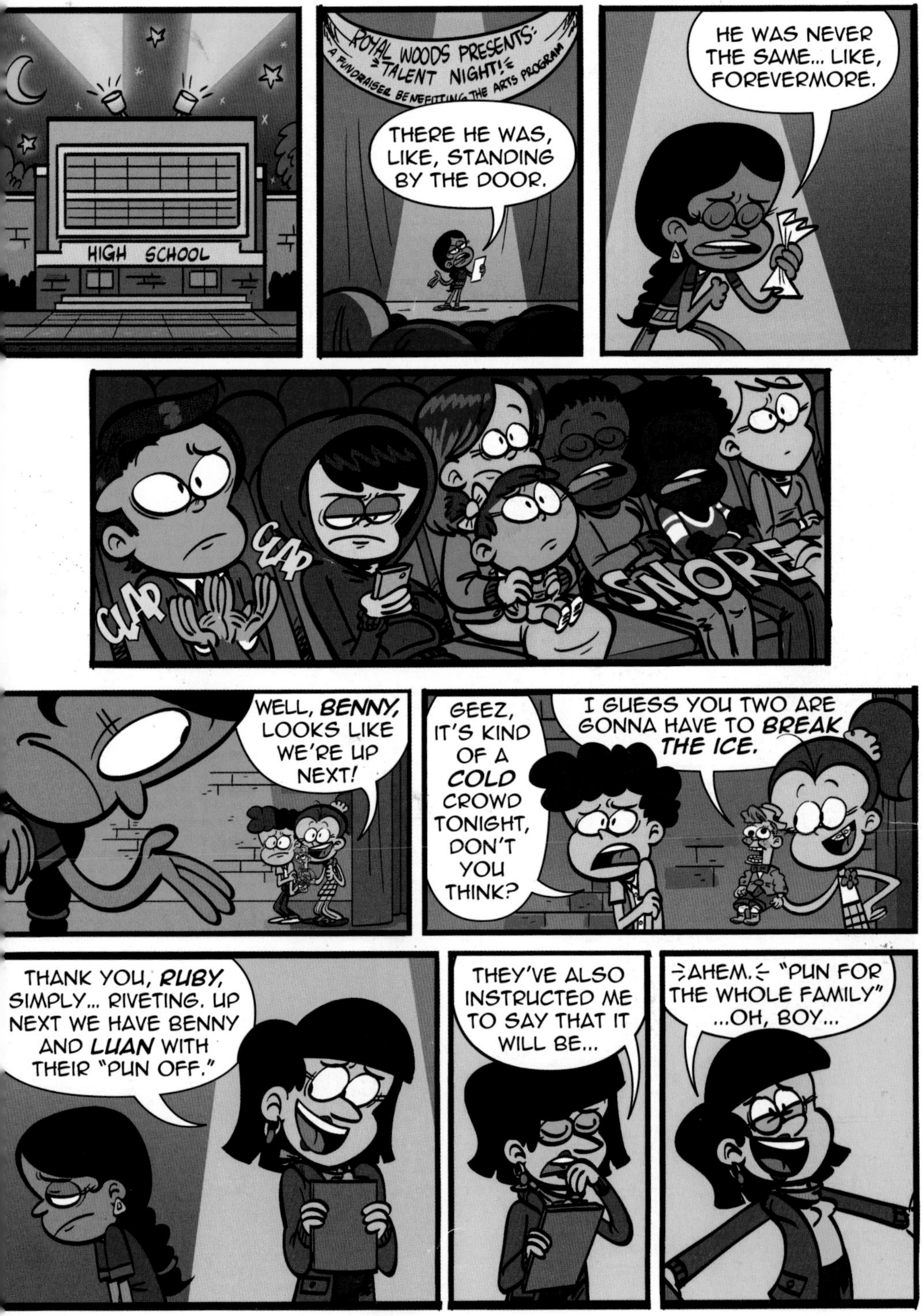
HIGH SCHOOL
ROYAL WOODS PRESENTS: TALENT NIGHT!
A FUNDRAISER BENEFITTING THE ARTS PROGRAM
THERE HE WAS, LIKE, STANDING BY THE DOOR.
HE WAS NEVER THE SAME... LIKE, FOREVERMORE.
CLAP
CLAP
CLAP
SNORE
WELL, **BENNY,** LOOKS LIKE WE'RE UP NEXT!
GEEZ, IT'S KIND OF A **COLD** CROWD TONIGHT, DON'T YOU THINK?
I GUESS YOU TWO ARE GONNA HAVE TO **BREAK THE ICE.**
THANK YOU, **RUBY,** SIMPLY... RIVETING. UP NEXT WE HAVE BENNY AND **LUAN** WITH THEIR "PUN OFF."
THEY'VE ALSO INSTRUCTED ME TO SAY THAT IT WILL BE...
AHEM. "PUN FOR THE WHOLE FAMILY" ...OH, BOY...

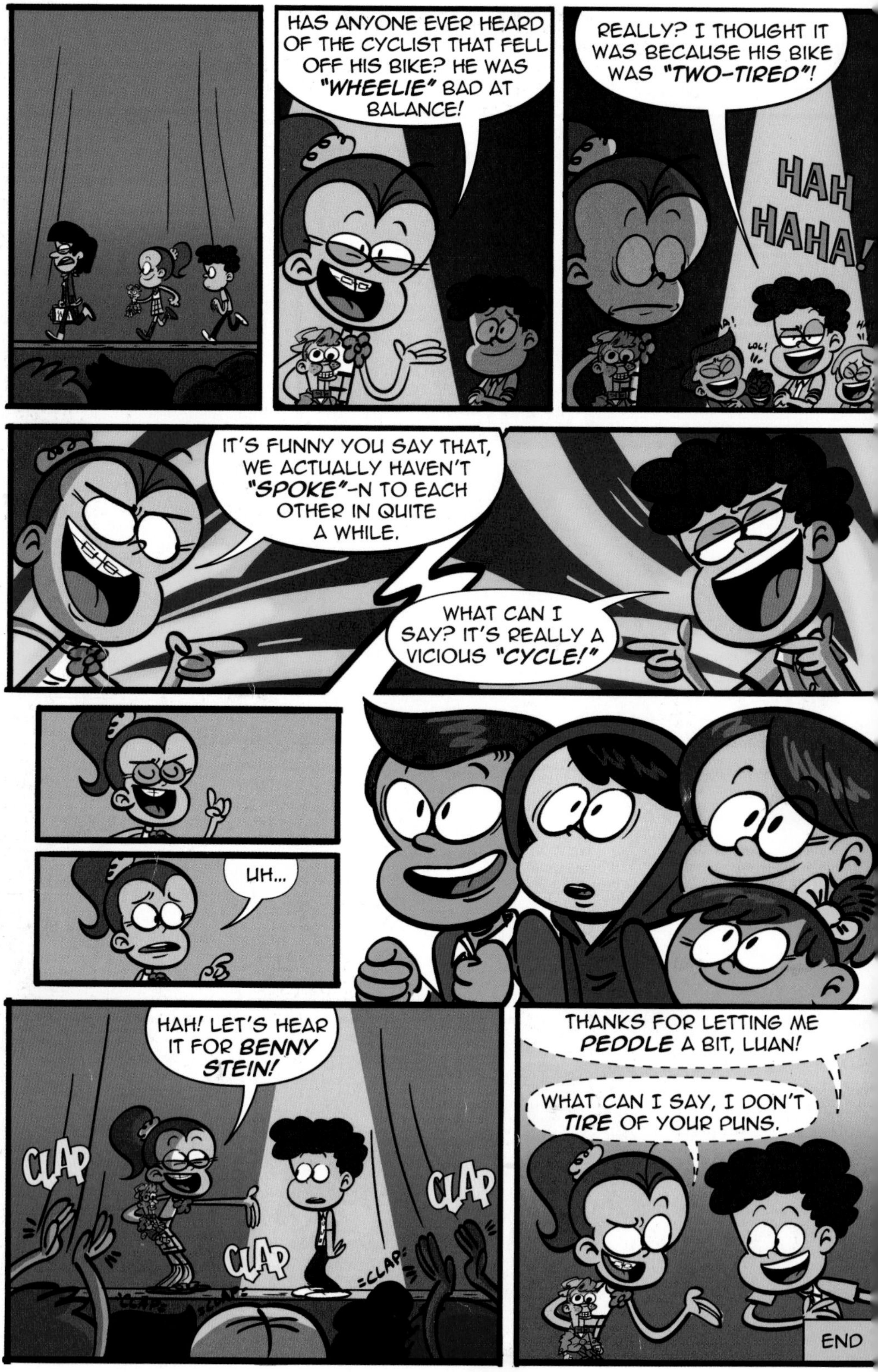
HAS ANYONE EVER HEARD OF THE CYCLIST THAT FELL OFF HIS BIKE? HE WAS "WHEELIE" BAD AT BALANCE!
REALLY? I THOUGHT IT WAS BECAUSE HIS BIKE WAS "TWO-TIRED"!
HAH HAHA!
LOL!
IT'S FUNNY YOU SAY THAT, WE ACTUALLY HAVEN'T "SPOKE"-N TO EACH OTHER IN QUITE A WHILE.
WHAT CAN I SAY? IT'S REALLY A VICIOUS "CYCLE!"
UH...
HAH! LET'S HEAR IT FOR BENNY STEIN!
CLAP
CLAP
CLAP
CLAP
THANKS FOR LETTING ME PEDDLE A BIT, LUAN!
WHAT CAN I SAY, I DON'T TIRE OF YOUR PUNS.
END

"SIR RIBBIT"

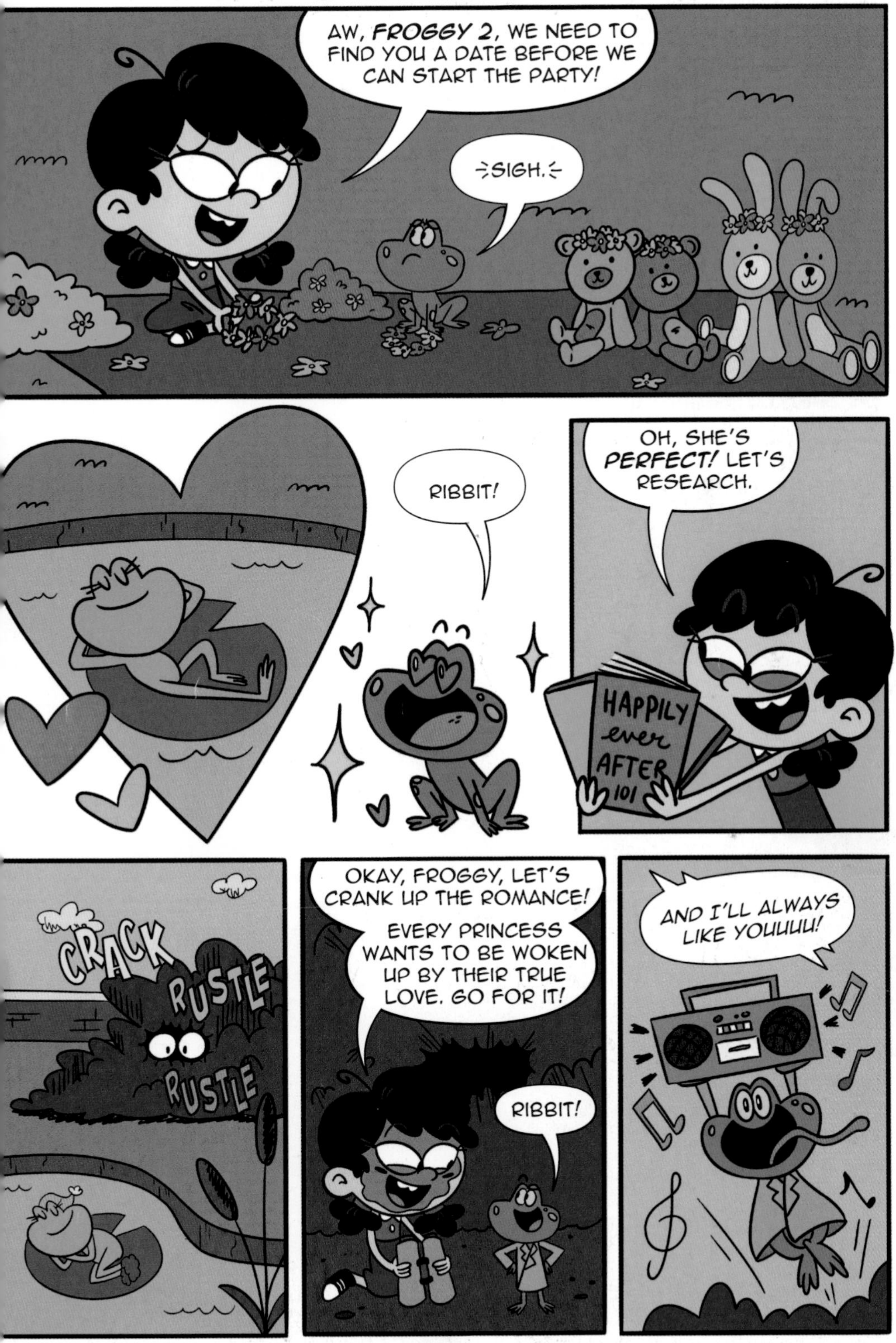

AW, FROGGY 2, WE NEED TO FIND YOU A DATE BEFORE WE CAN START THE PARTY!
SIGH.
RIBBIT!
OH, SHE'S PERFECT! LET'S RESEARCH.
HAPPILY ever AFTER 101
CRACK
RUSTLE
RUSTLE
OKAY, FROGGY, LET'S CRANK UP THE ROMANCE!
EVERY PRINCESS WANTS TO BE WOKEN UP BY THEIR TRUE LOVE. GO FOR IT!
RIBBIT!
AND I'LL ALWAYS LIKE YOUUUU!

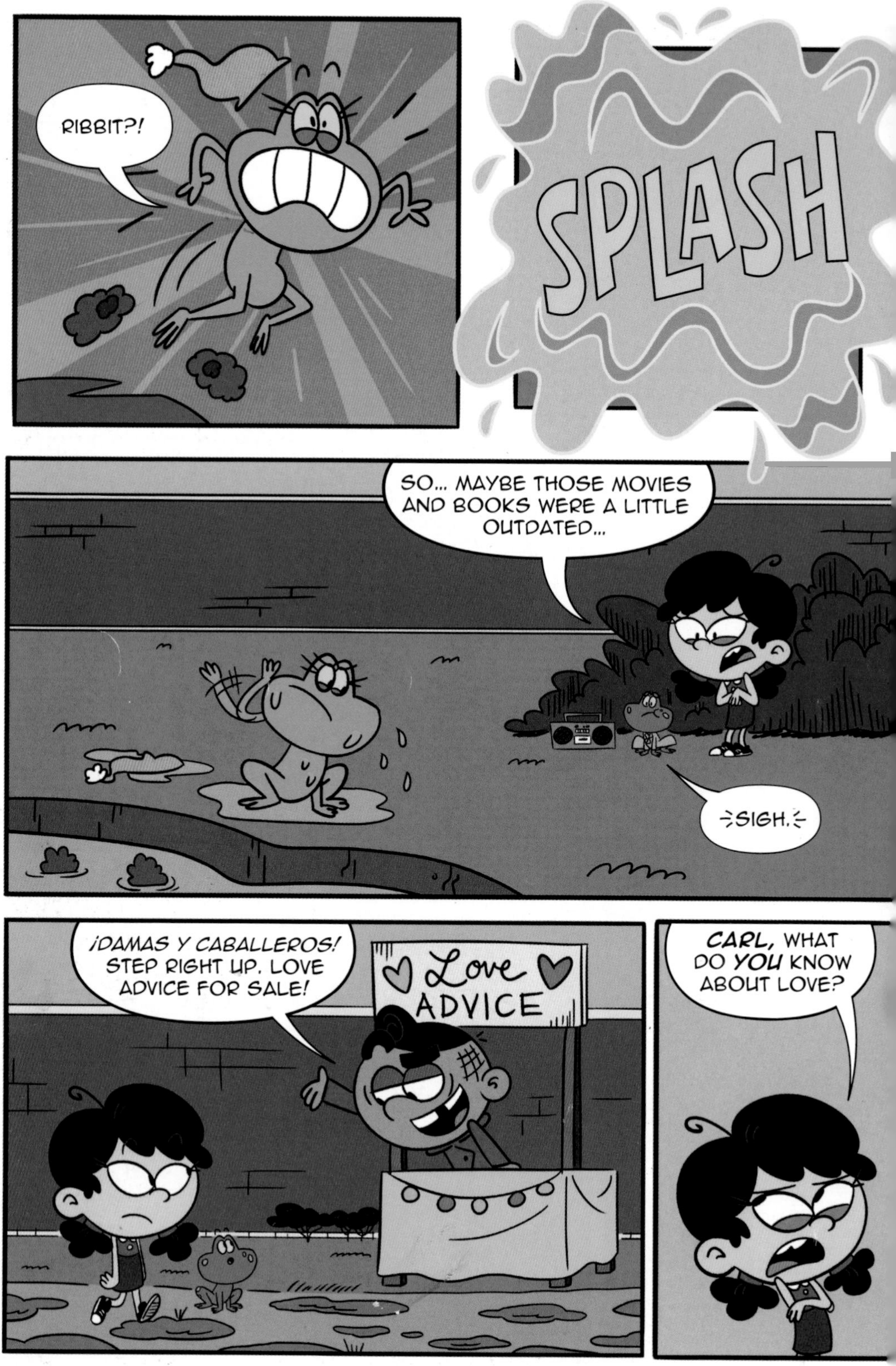
RIBBIT?!
SPLASH
SO... MAYBE THOSE MOVIES AND BOOKS WERE A LITTLE OUTDATED...
≈SIGH.≈
¡DAMAS Y CABALLEROS! STEP RIGHT UP. LOVE ADVICE FOR SALE!
Love ADVICE
CARL, WHAT DO YOU KNOW ABOUT LOVE?

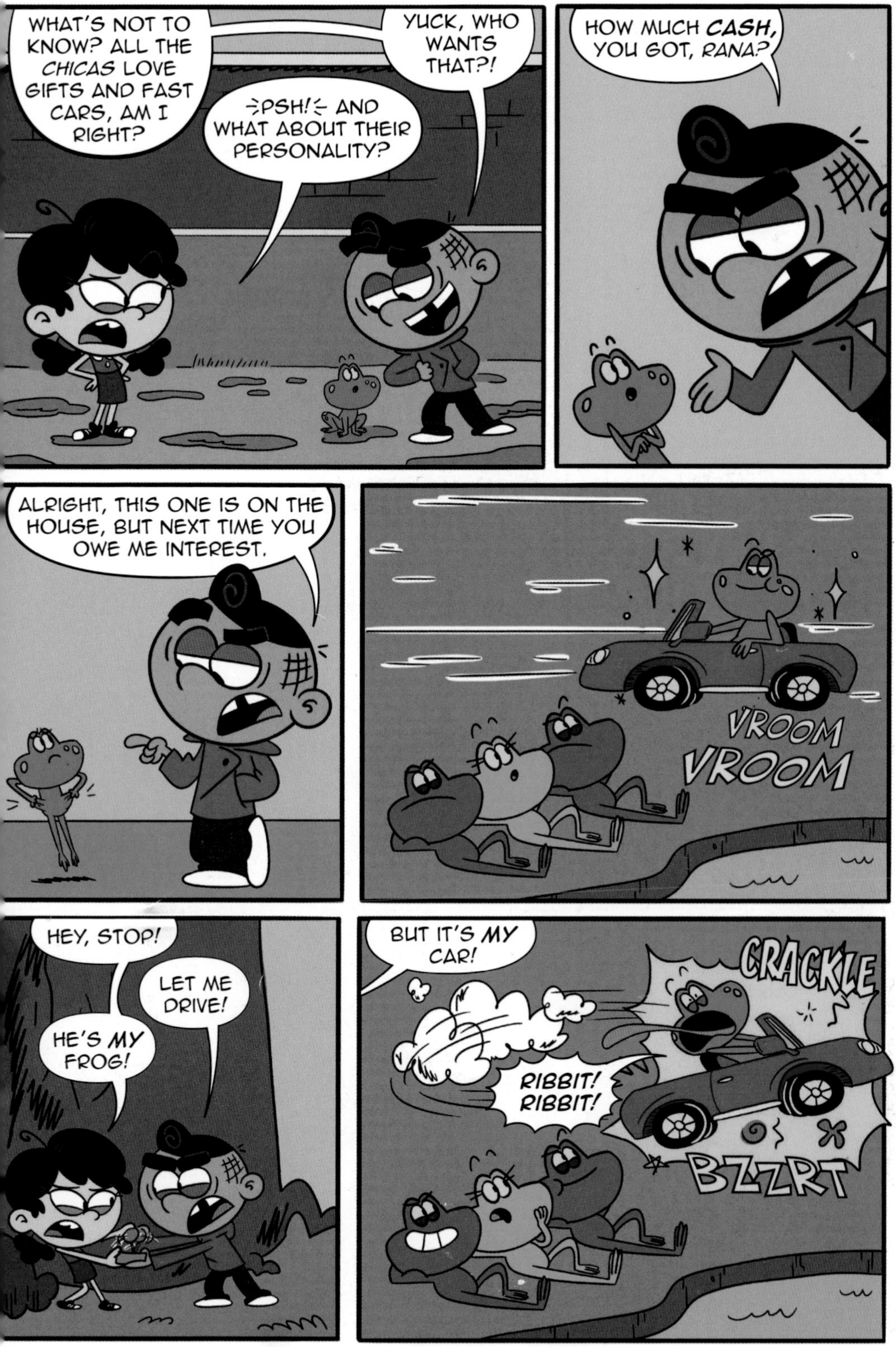
WHAT'S NOT TO KNOW? ALL THE CHICAS LOVE GIFTS AND FAST CARS, AM I RIGHT?
YUCK, WHO WANTS THAT?!
PSH! AND WHAT ABOUT THEIR PERSONALITY?
HOW MUCH CASH, YOU GOT, RANA?
ALRIGHT, THIS ONE IS ON THE HOUSE, BUT NEXT TIME YOU OWE ME INTEREST.
VROOM VROOM
HEY, STOP!
LET ME DRIVE!
HE'S MY FROG!
BUT IT'S MY CAR!
CRACKLE
RIBBIT! RIBBIT!
BZZRT

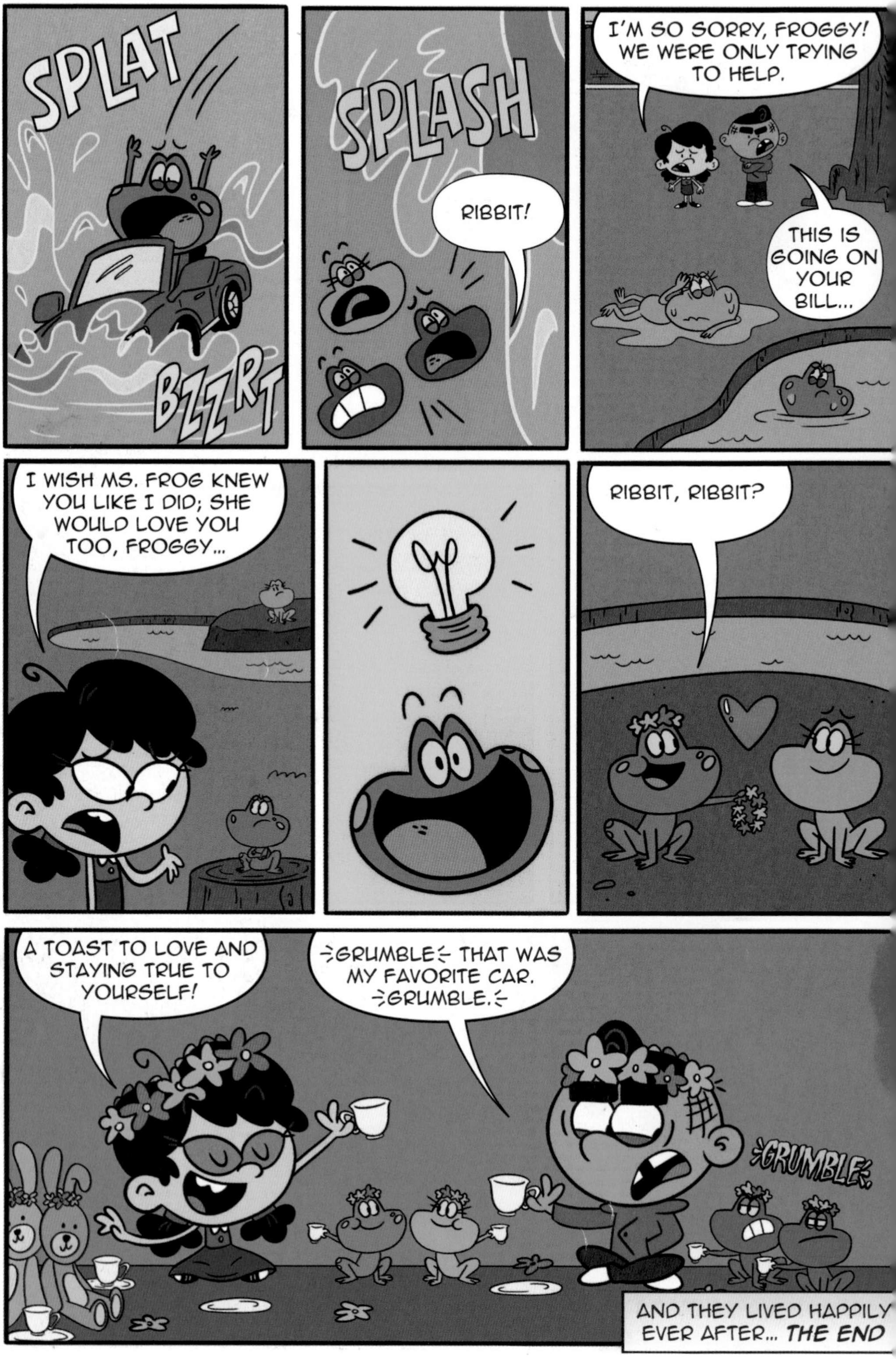
SPLAT
BZZRT
SPLASH
RIBBIT!
I'M SO SORRY, FROGGY! WE WERE ONLY TRYING TO HELP.
THIS IS GOING ON YOUR BILL...
I WISH MS. FROG KNEW YOU LIKE I DID; SHE WOULD LOVE YOU TOO, FROGGY...
RIBBIT, RIBBIT?
A TOAST TO LOVE AND STAYING TRUE TO YOURSELF!
GRUMBLE THAT WAS MY FAVORITE CAR. GRUMBLE.
GRUMBLE
AND THEY LIVED HAPPILY EVER AFTER... THE END

"TIME TO RHYME"

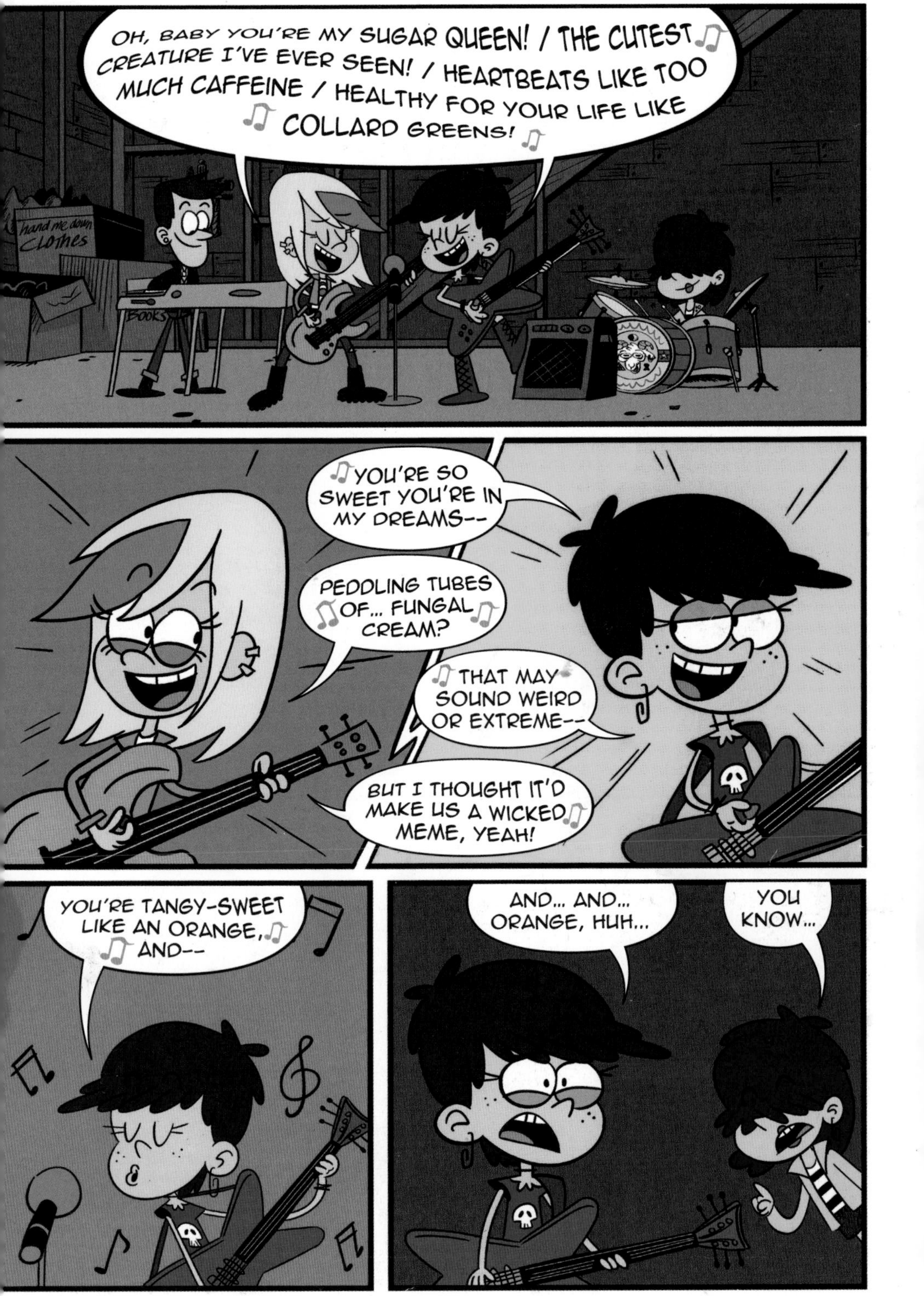
OH, BABY YOU'RE MY SUGAR QUEEN! / THE CUTEST CREATURE I'VE EVER SEEN! / HEARTBEATS LIKE TOO MUCH CAFFEINE / HEALTHY FOR YOUR LIFE LIKE COLLARD GREENS!
hand me down Clothes
BOOKS
YOU'RE SO SWEET YOU'RE IN MY DREAMS--
PEDDLING TUBES OF... FUNGAL CREAM?
THAT MAY SOUND WEIRD OR EXTREME--
BUT I THOUGHT IT'D MAKE US A WICKED MEME, YEAH!
YOU'RE TANGY-SWEET LIKE AN ORANGE, AND--
AND... AND... ORANGE, HUH...
YOU KNOW...

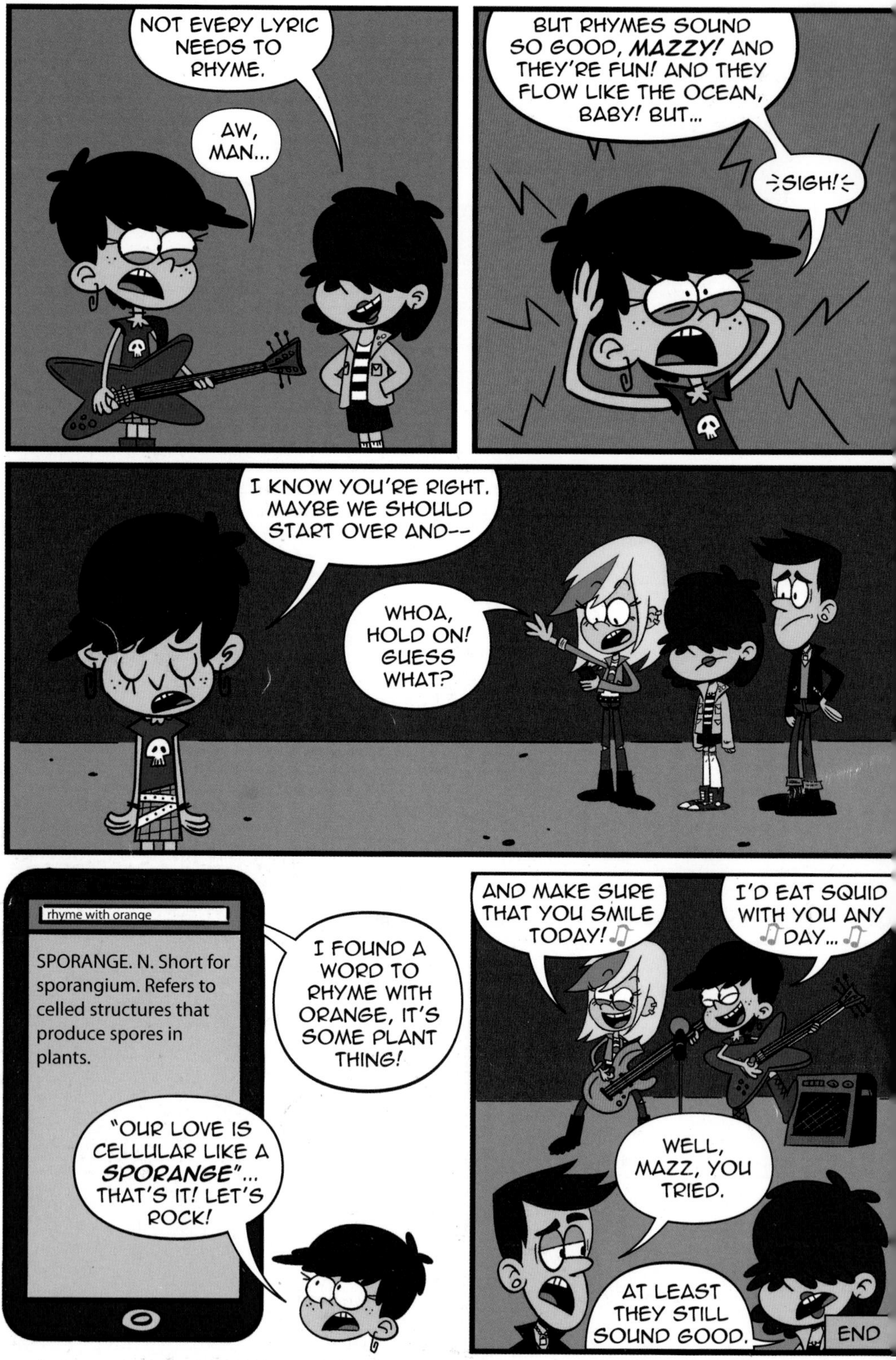
NOT EVERY LYRIC NEEDS TO RHYME.
AW, MAN...
BUT RHYMES SOUND SO GOOD, *MAZZY!* AND THEY'RE FUN! AND THEY FLOW LIKE THE OCEAN, BABY! BUT...
SIGH!
I KNOW YOU'RE RIGHT. MAYBE WE SHOULD START OVER AND--
WHOA, HOLD ON! GUESS WHAT?
rhyme with orange
SPORANGE. N. Short for sporangium. Refers to celled structures that produce spores in plants.
I FOUND A WORD TO RHYME WITH ORANGE, IT'S SOME PLANT THING!
"OUR LOVE IS CELLULAR LIKE A *SPORANGE*"... THAT'S IT! LET'S ROCK!
AND MAKE SURE THAT YOU SMILE TODAY!
I'D EAT SQUID WITH YOU ANY DAY...
WELL, MAZZ, YOU TRIED.
AT LEAST THEY STILL SOUND GOOD.
END

"HAPPY PLAN-IVERSARY"

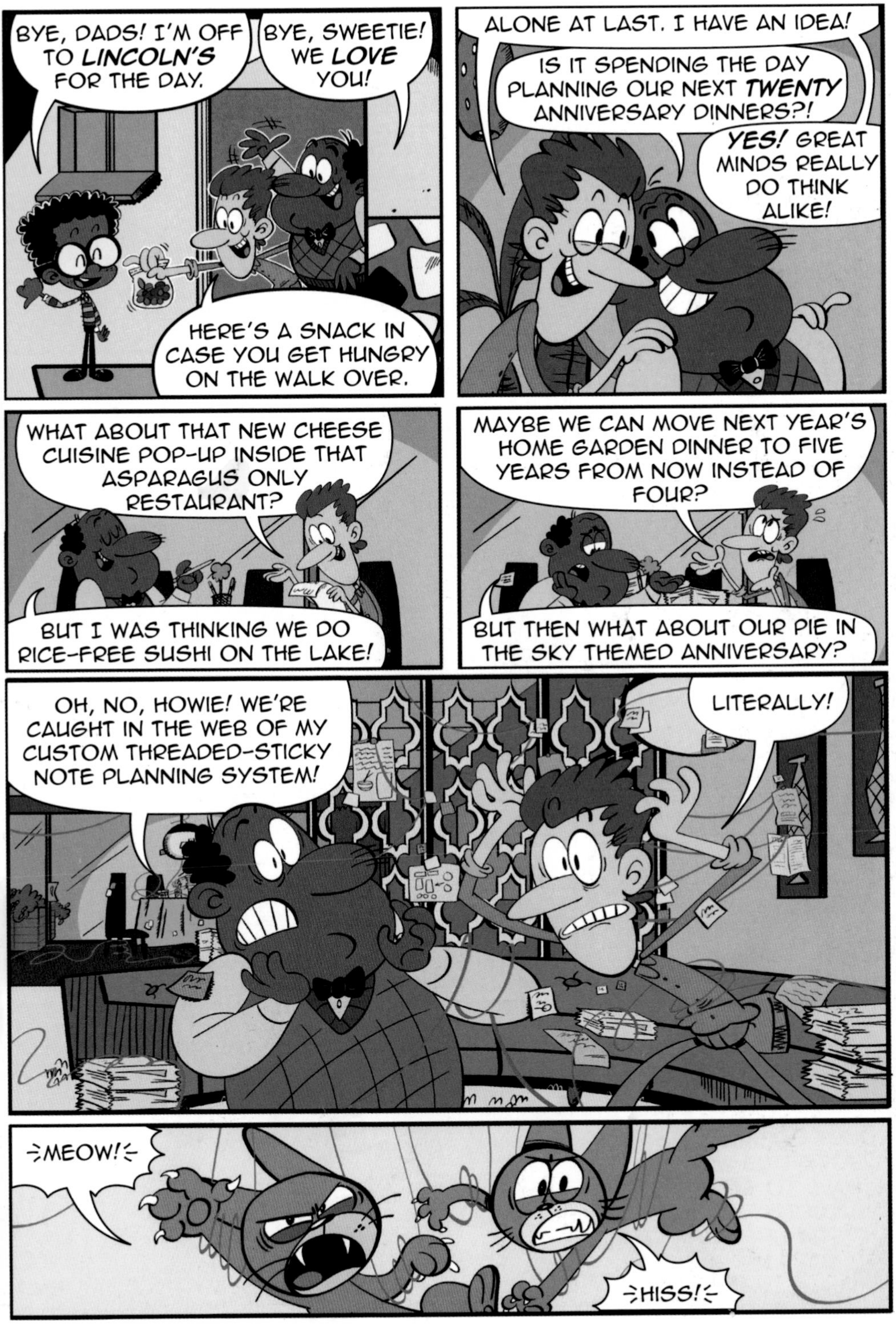

BYE, DADS! I'M OFF TO LINCOLN'S FOR THE DAY.
BYE, SWEETIE! WE LOVE YOU!
HERE'S A SNACK IN CASE YOU GET HUNGRY ON THE WALK OVER.
ALONE AT LAST. I HAVE AN IDEA!
IS IT SPENDING THE DAY PLANNING OUR NEXT TWENTY ANNIVERSARY DINNERS?!
YES! GREAT MINDS REALLY DO THINK ALIKE!
WHAT ABOUT THAT NEW CHEESE CUISINE POP-UP INSIDE THAT ASPARAGUS ONLY RESTAURANT?
BUT I WAS THINKING WE DO RICE-FREE SUSHI ON THE LAKE!
MAYBE WE CAN MOVE NEXT YEAR'S HOME GARDEN DINNER TO FIVE YEARS FROM NOW INSTEAD OF FOUR?
BUT THEN WHAT ABOUT OUR PIE IN THE SKY THEMED ANNIVERSARY?
OH, NO, HOWIE! WE'RE CAUGHT IN THE WEB OF MY CUSTOM THREADED-STICKY NOTE PLANNING SYSTEM!
LITERALLY!
MEOW!
HISS!

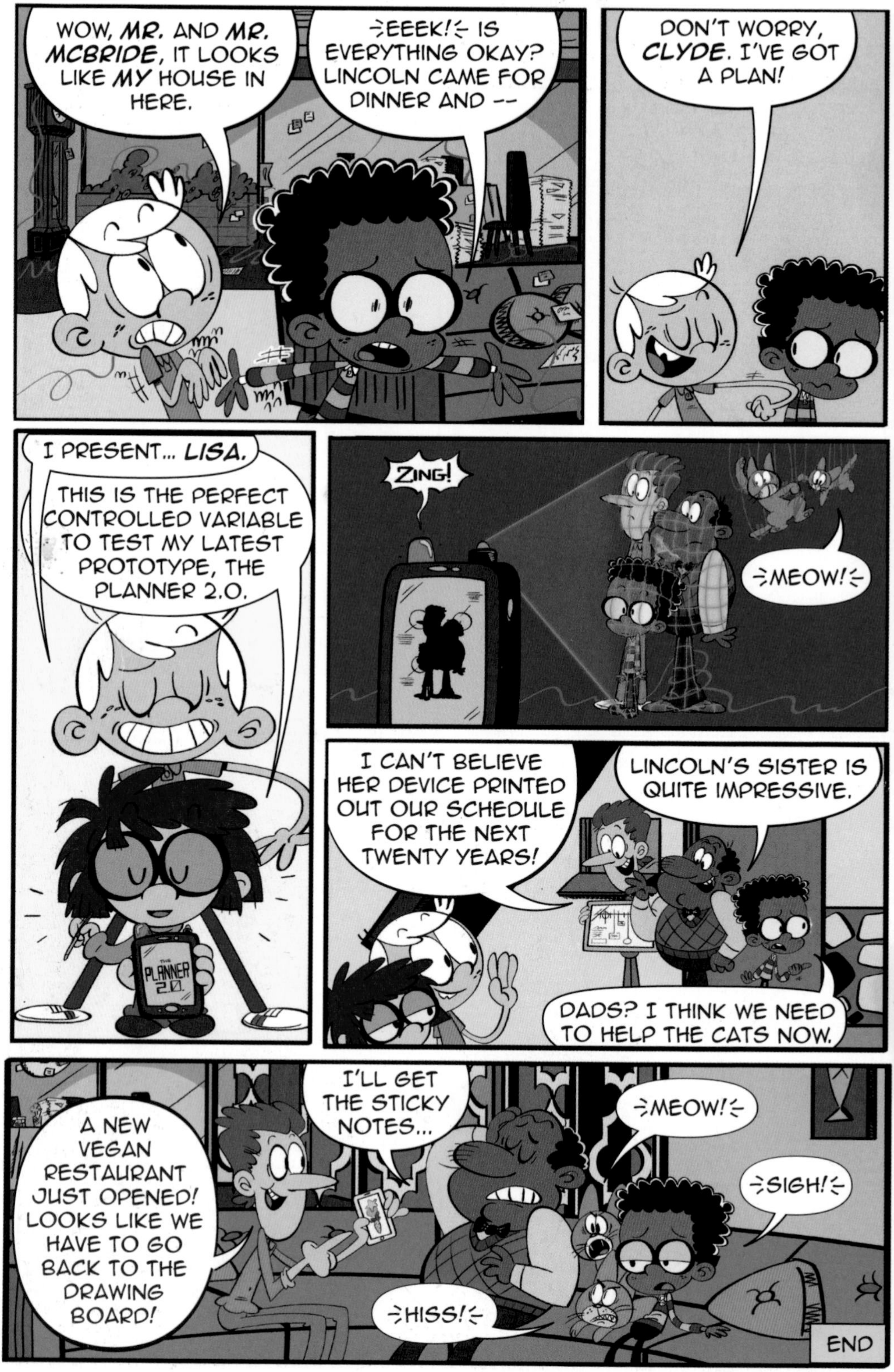
WOW, MR. AND MR. MCBRIDE, IT LOOKS LIKE MY HOUSE IN HERE.
EEEK! IS EVERYTHING OKAY? LINCOLN CAME FOR DINNER AND --
DON'T WORRY, CLYDE. I'VE GOT A PLAN!
I PRESENT... LISA.
THIS IS THE PERFECT CONTROLLED VARIABLE TO TEST MY LATEST PROTOTYPE, THE PLANNER 2.0.
THE PLANNER 2.0
ZING!
MEOW!
I CAN'T BELIEVE HER DEVICE PRINTED OUT OUR SCHEDULE FOR THE NEXT TWENTY YEARS!
LINCOLN'S SISTER IS QUITE IMPRESSIVE.
DADS? I THINK WE NEED TO HELP THE CATS NOW.
A NEW VEGAN RESTAURANT JUST OPENED! LOOKS LIKE WE HAVE TO GO BACK TO THE DRAWING BOARD!
I'LL GET THE STICKY NOTES...
MEOW!
SIGH!
HISS!
END

"BEAR HUG"

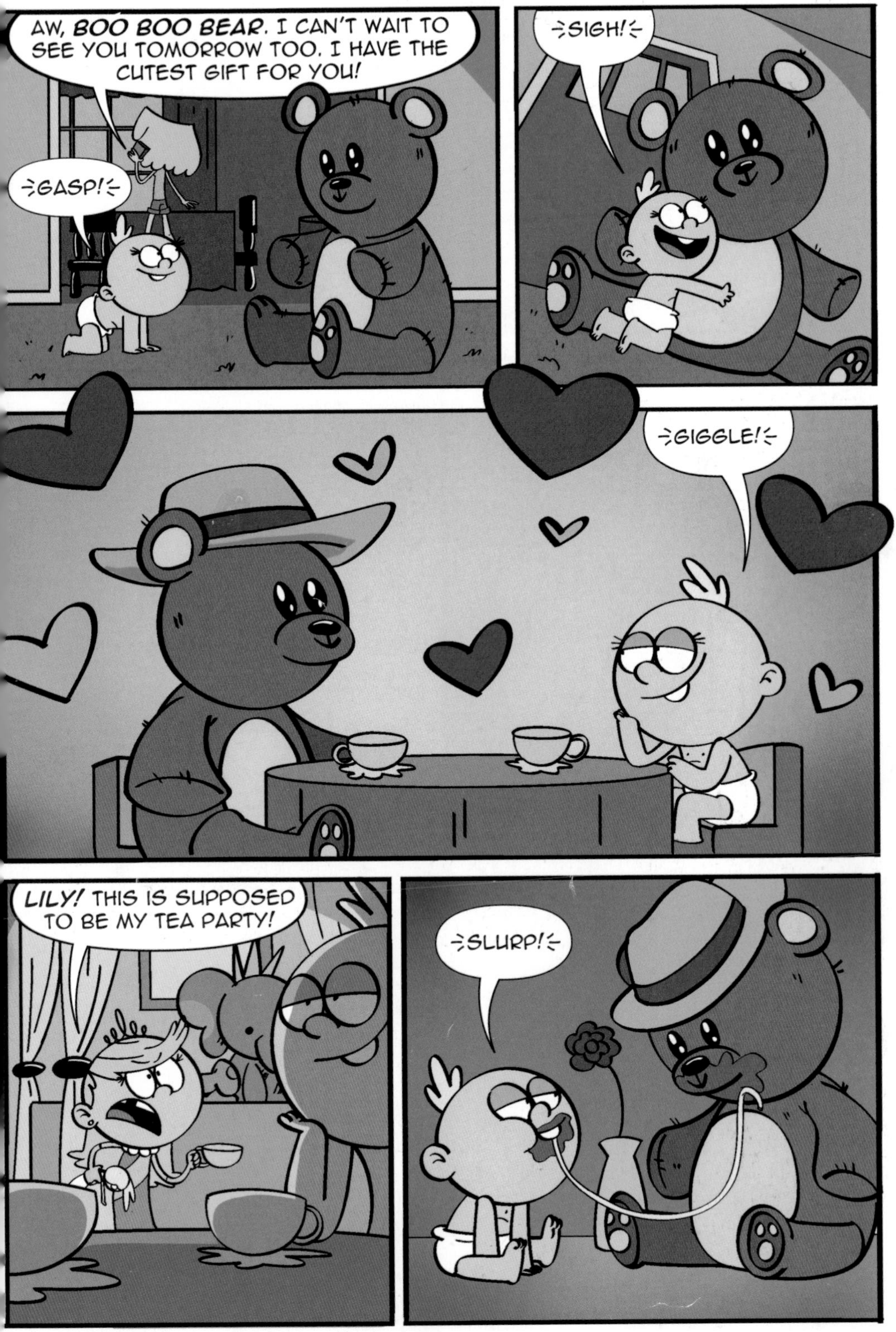
AW, BOO BOO BEAR. I CAN'T WAIT TO SEE YOU TOMORROW TOO. I HAVE THE CUTEST GIFT FOR YOU!
GASP!
SIGH!
GIGGLE!
LILY! THIS IS SUPPOSED TO BE MY TEA PARTY!
SLURP!

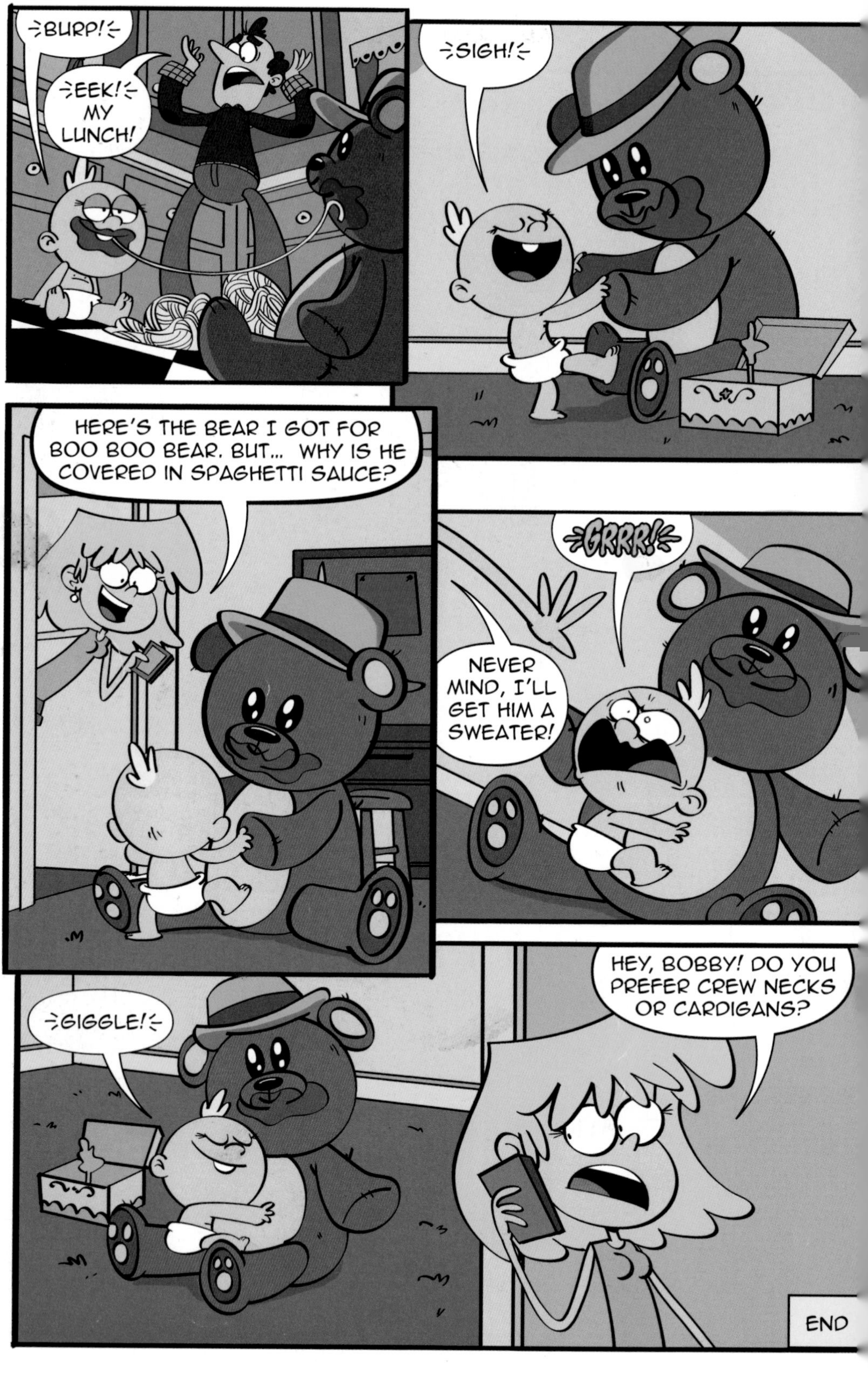
BURP!
EEK! MY LUNCH!
SIGH!
HERE'S THE BEAR I GOT FOR BOO BOO BEAR. BUT... WHY IS HE COVERED IN SPAGHETTI SAUCE?
GRRR!
NEVER MIND, I'LL GET HIM A SWEATER!
GIGGLE!
HEY, BOBBY! DO YOU PREFER CREW NECKS OR CARDIGANS?
END

"BOA ON BOARD"

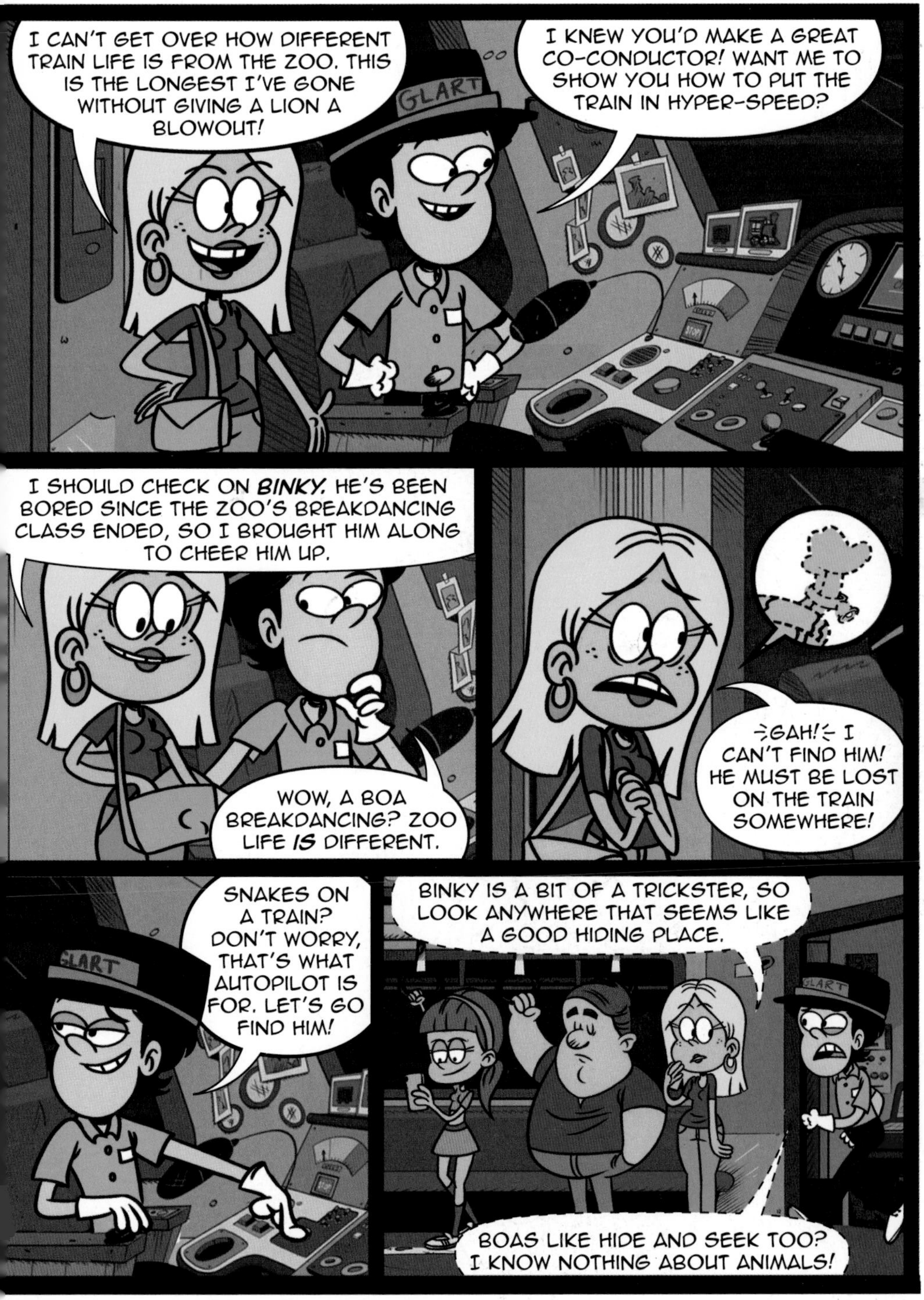
I CAN'T GET OVER HOW DIFFERENT TRAIN LIFE IS FROM THE ZOO. THIS IS THE LONGEST I'VE GONE WITHOUT GIVING A LION A BLOWOUT!
GLART
I KNEW YOU'D MAKE A GREAT CO-CONDUCTOR! WANT ME TO SHOW YOU HOW TO PUT THE TRAIN IN HYPER-SPEED?
STOP
I SHOULD CHECK ON BINKY. HE'S BEEN BORED SINCE THE ZOO'S BREAKDANCING CLASS ENDED, SO I BROUGHT HIM ALONG TO CHEER HIM UP.
WOW, A BOA BREAKDANCING? ZOO LIFE IS DIFFERENT.
GAH! I CAN'T FIND HIM! HE MUST BE LOST ON THE TRAIN SOMEWHERE!
GLART
SNAKES ON A TRAIN? DON'T WORRY, THAT'S WHAT AUTOPILOT IS FOR. LET'S GO FIND HIM!
BINKY IS A BIT OF A TRICKSTER, SO LOOK ANYWHERE THAT SEEMS LIKE A GOOD HIDING PLACE.
GLART
BOAS LIKE HIDE AND SEEK TOO? I KNOW NOTHING ABOUT ANIMALS!

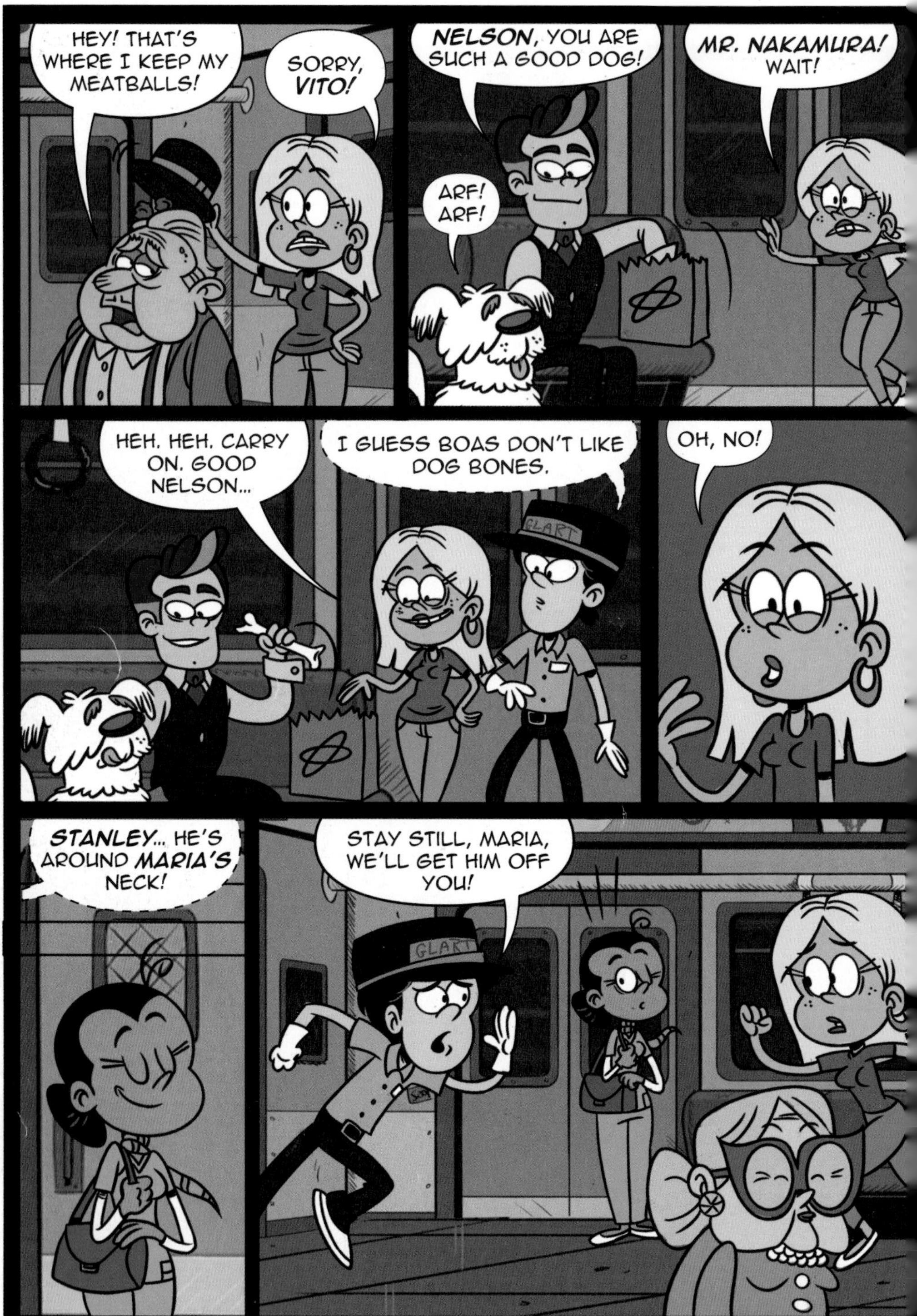
HEY! THAT'S WHERE I KEEP MY MEATBALLS!
SORRY, VITO!
NELSON, YOU ARE SUCH A GOOD DOG!
ARF! ARF!
MR. NAKAMURA! WAIT!
HEH. HEH. CARRY ON. GOOD NELSON...
I GUESS BOAS DON'T LIKE DOG BONES.
GLART
OH, NO!
STANLEY... HE'S AROUND MARIA'S NECK!
STAY STILL, MARIA, WE'LL GET HIM OFF YOU!
GLART

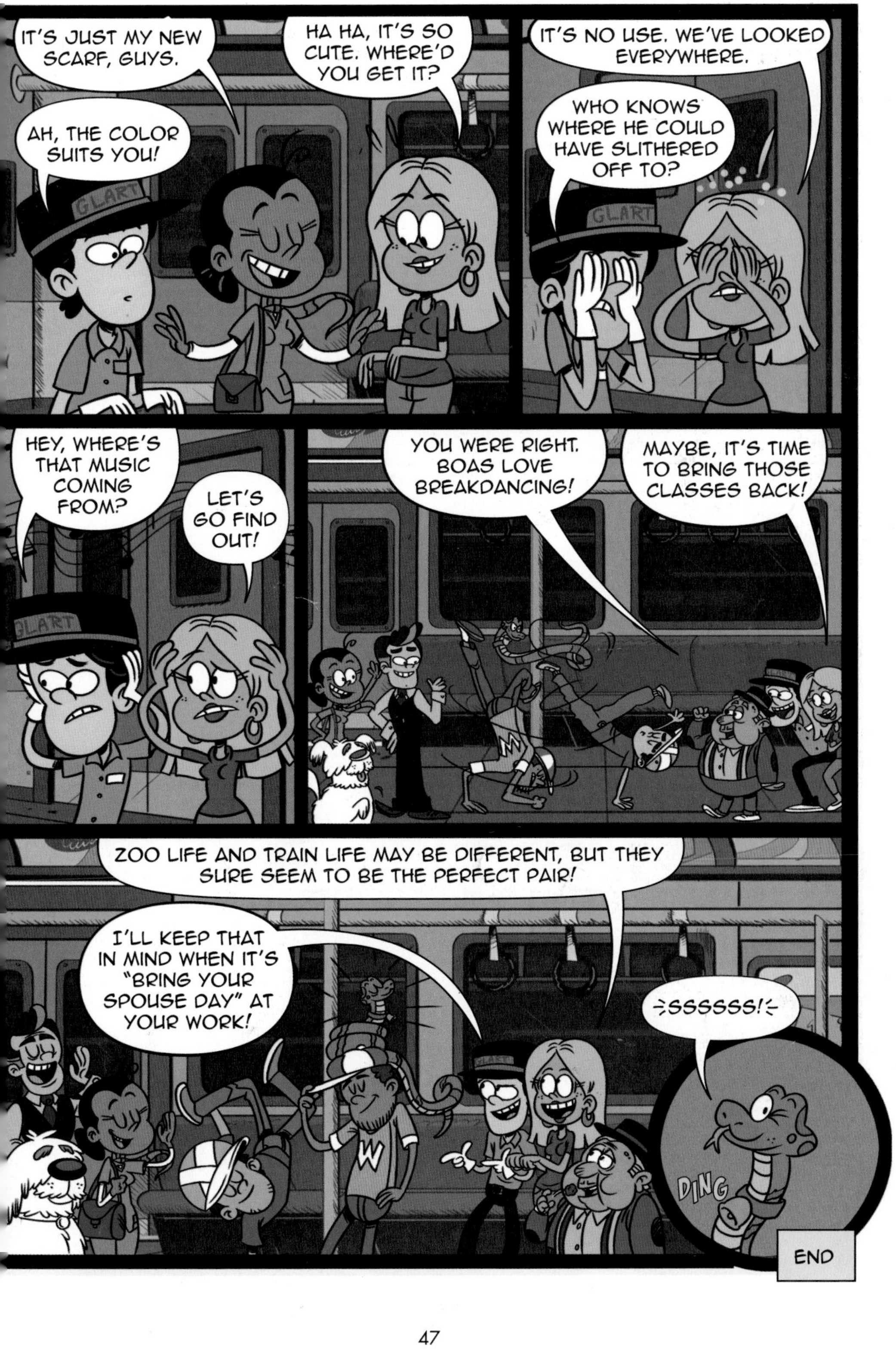
IT'S JUST MY NEW SCARF, GUYS.
AH, THE COLOR SUITS YOU!
HA HA, IT'S SO CUTE. WHERE'D YOU GET IT?
IT'S NO USE. WE'VE LOOKED EVERYWHERE.
WHO KNOWS WHERE HE COULD HAVE SLITHERED OFF TO?
GLART
HEY, WHERE'S THAT MUSIC COMING FROM?
LET'S GO FIND OUT!
YOU WERE RIGHT. BOAS LOVE BREAKDANCING!
MAYBE, IT'S TIME TO BRING THOSE CLASSES BACK!
ZOO LIFE AND TRAIN LIFE MAY BE DIFFERENT, BUT THEY SURE SEEM TO BE THE PERFECT PAIR!
I'LL KEEP THAT IN MIND WHEN IT'S "BRING YOUR SPOUSE DAY" AT YOUR WORK!
SSSSSS!
DING
END

"CAFÉ CONFUSION"

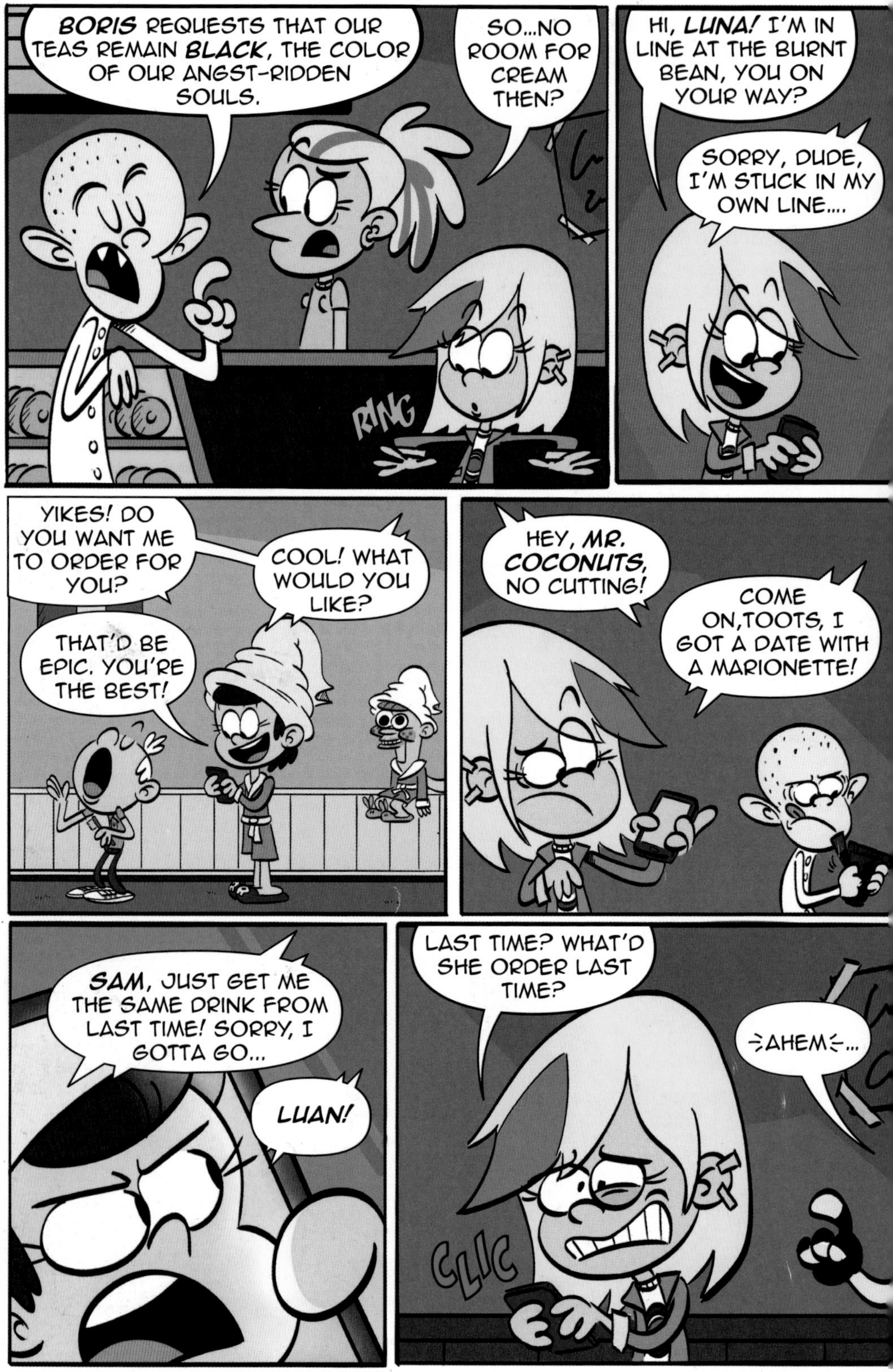
BORIS REQUESTS THAT OUR TEAS REMAIN BLACK, THE COLOR OF OUR ANGST-RIDDEN SOULS.
SO...NO ROOM FOR CREAM THEN?
RING
HI, LUNA! I'M IN LINE AT THE BURNT BEAN, YOU ON YOUR WAY?
SORRY, DUDE, I'M STUCK IN MY OWN LINE....
YIKES! DO YOU WANT ME TO ORDER FOR YOU?
COOL! WHAT WOULD YOU LIKE?
THAT'D BE EPIC. YOU'RE THE BEST!
HEY, MR. COCONUTS, NO CUTTING!
COME ON,TOOTS, I GOT A DATE WITH A MARIONETTE!
SAM, JUST GET ME THE SAME DRINK FROM LAST TIME! SORRY, I GOTTA GO...
LUAN!
LAST TIME? WHAT'D SHE ORDER LAST TIME?
AHEM...
CLIC

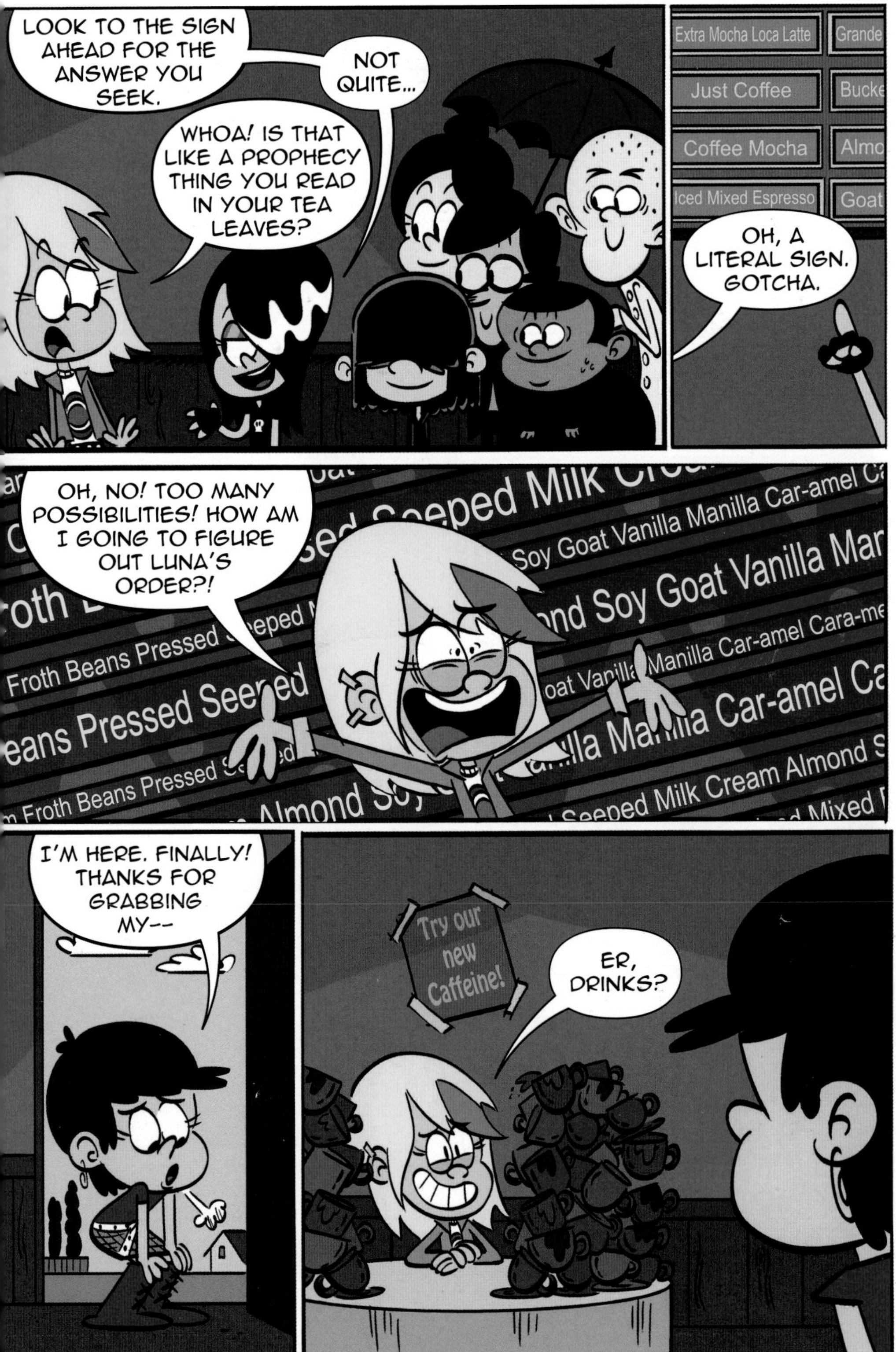
LOOK TO THE SIGN AHEAD FOR THE ANSWER YOU SEEK.
NOT QUITE...
WHOA! IS THAT LIKE A PROPHECY THING YOU READ IN YOUR TEA LEAVES?
Extra Mocha Loca Latte
Grande
Just Coffee
Coffee Mocha
Iced Mixed Espresso
Goat
OH, A LITERAL SIGN. GOTCHA.
OH, NO! TOO MANY POSSIBILITIES! HOW AM I GOING TO FIGURE OUT LUNA'S ORDER?!
Soy Goat Vanilla Manilla Car-amel
Froth Beans Pressed
Beans Pressed
Manilla Car-amel Cara-me
Seeped Milk Cream Almond
I'M HERE. FINALLY! THANKS FOR GRABBING MY--
Try our new Caffeine!
ER, DRINKS?

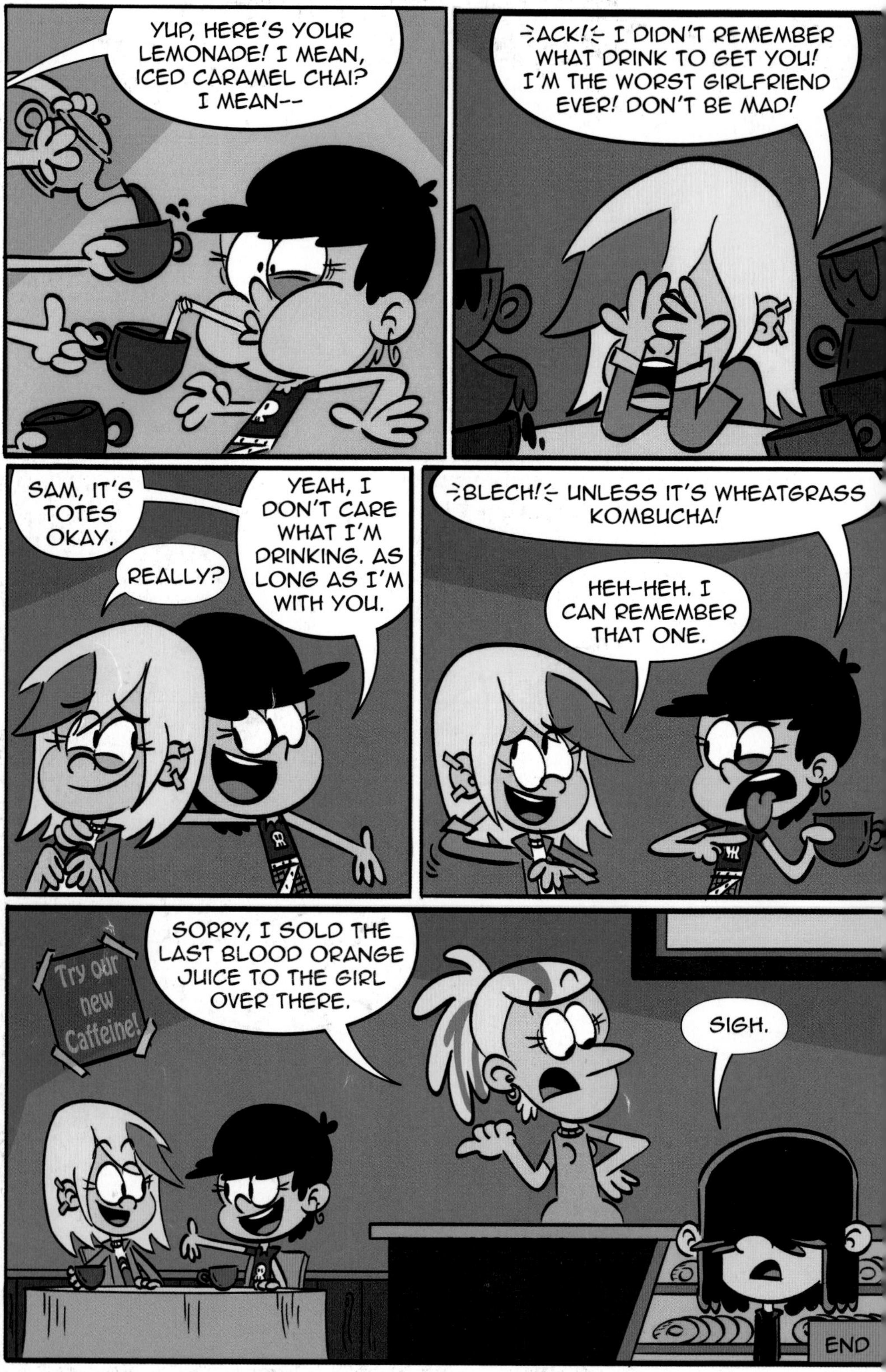
YUP, HERE'S YOUR LEMONADE! I MEAN, ICED CARAMEL CHAI? I MEAN--
ACK! I DIDN'T REMEMBER WHAT DRINK TO GET YOU! I'M THE WORST GIRLFRIEND EVER! DON'T BE MAD!
SAM, IT'S TOTES OKAY.
YEAH, I DON'T CARE WHAT I'M DRINKING. AS LONG AS I'M WITH YOU.
REALLY?
BLECH! UNLESS IT'S WHEATGRASS KOMBUCHA!
HEH-HEH. I CAN REMEMBER THAT ONE.
Try our new Caffeine!
SORRY, I SOLD THE LAST BLOOD ORANGE JUICE TO THE GIRL OVER THERE.
SIGH.
END

"MANIC MONDAY"

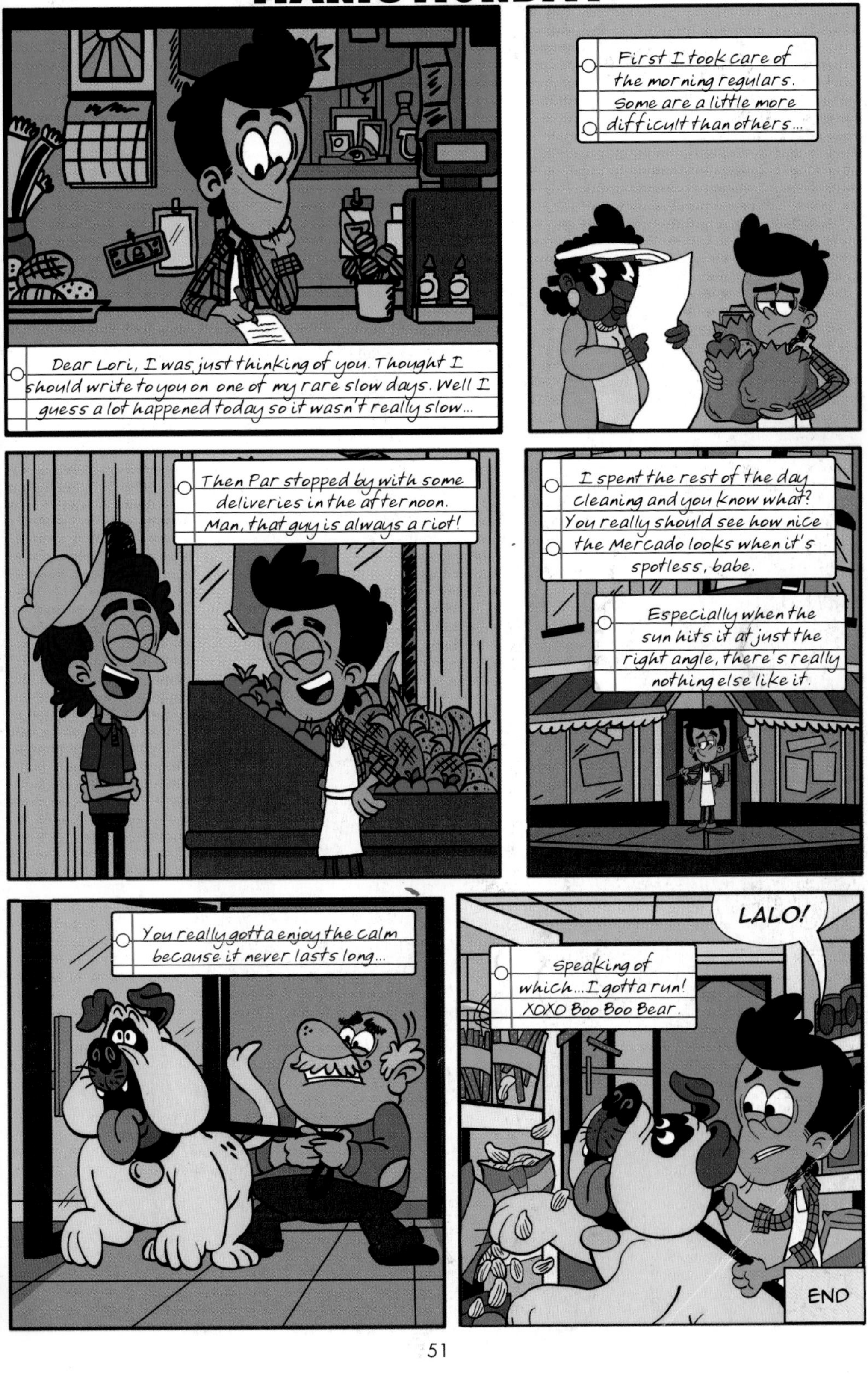
Dear Lori, I was just thinking of you. Thought I should write to you on one of my rare slow days. Well I guess a lot happened today so it wasn't really slow...
First I took care of the morning regulars. Some are a little more difficult than others...
Then Par stopped by with some deliveries in the afternoon. Man, that guy is always a riot!
I spent the rest of the day cleaning and you know what? You really should see how nice the Mercado looks when it's spotless, babe.
Especially when the sun hits it at just the right angle, there's really nothing else like it.
You really gotta enjoy the calm because it never lasts long...
LALO!
Speaking of which... I gotta run! XOXO Boo Boo Bear.
END

"FROM THE HEART"

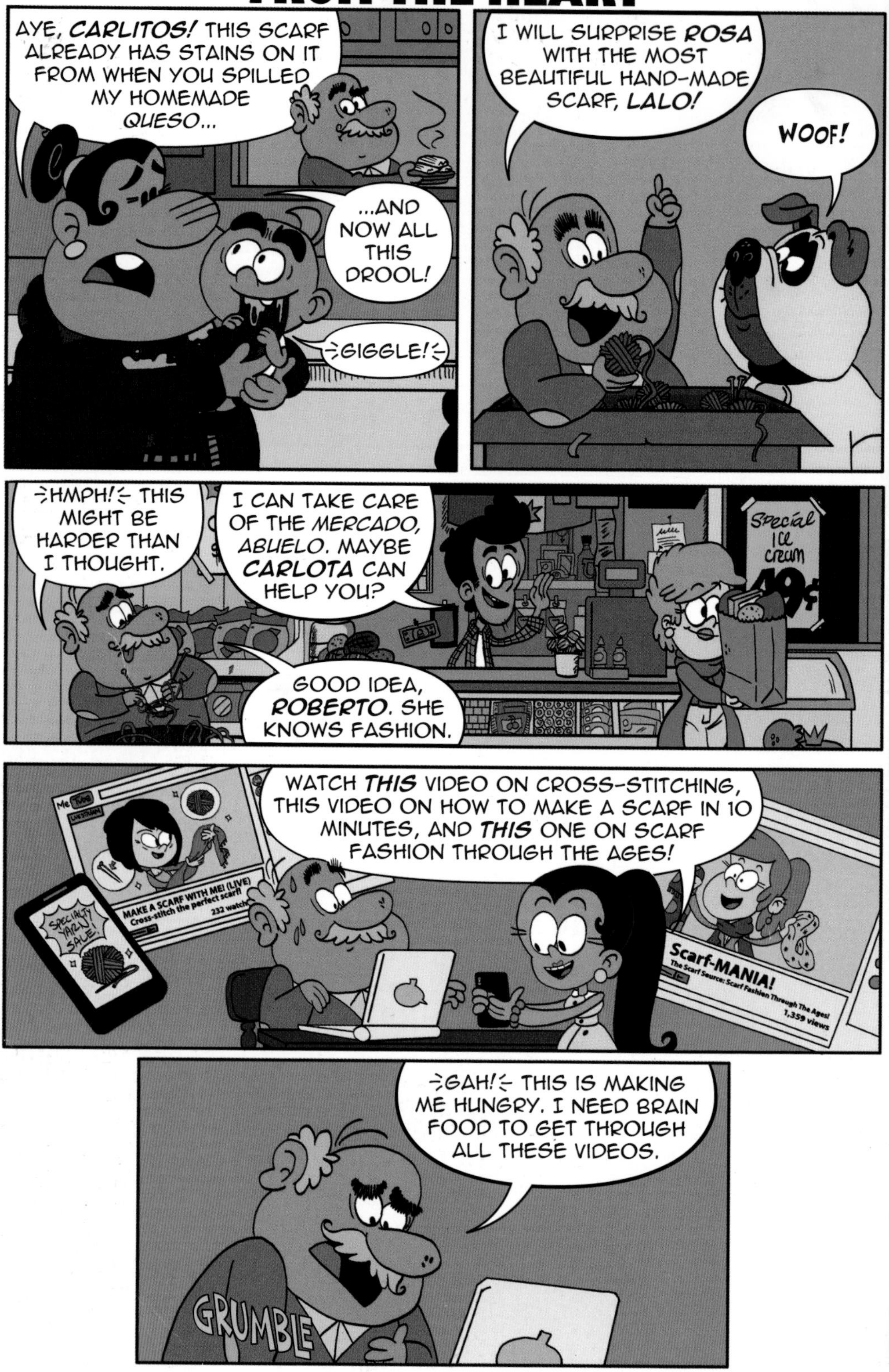

AYE, CARLITOS! THIS SCARF ALREADY HAS STAINS ON IT FROM WHEN YOU SPILLED MY HOMEMADE QUESO...
...AND NOW ALL THIS DROOL!
GIGGLE!
I WILL SURPRISE ROSA WITH THE MOST BEAUTIFUL HAND-MADE SCARF, LALO!
WOOF!
HMPH! THIS MIGHT BE HARDER THAN I THOUGHT.
I CAN TAKE CARE OF THE MERCADO, ABUELO. MAYBE CARLOTA CAN HELP YOU?
Special Ice Cream 49¢
GOOD IDEA, ROBERTO. SHE KNOWS FASHION.
WATCH THIS VIDEO ON CROSS-STITCHING, THIS VIDEO ON HOW TO MAKE A SCARF IN 10 MINUTES, AND THIS ONE ON SCARF FASHION THROUGH THE AGES!
MAKE A SCARF WITH ME! (LIVE)
Cross-stitch the perfect scarf!
SPECIALTY YARN SALE!
Scarf-MANIA!
The Scarf Source: Scarf Fashion Through The Ages!
1,359 views
GAH! THIS IS MAKING ME HUNGRY. I NEED BRAIN FOOD TO GET THROUGH ALL THESE VIDEOS.
GRUMBLE

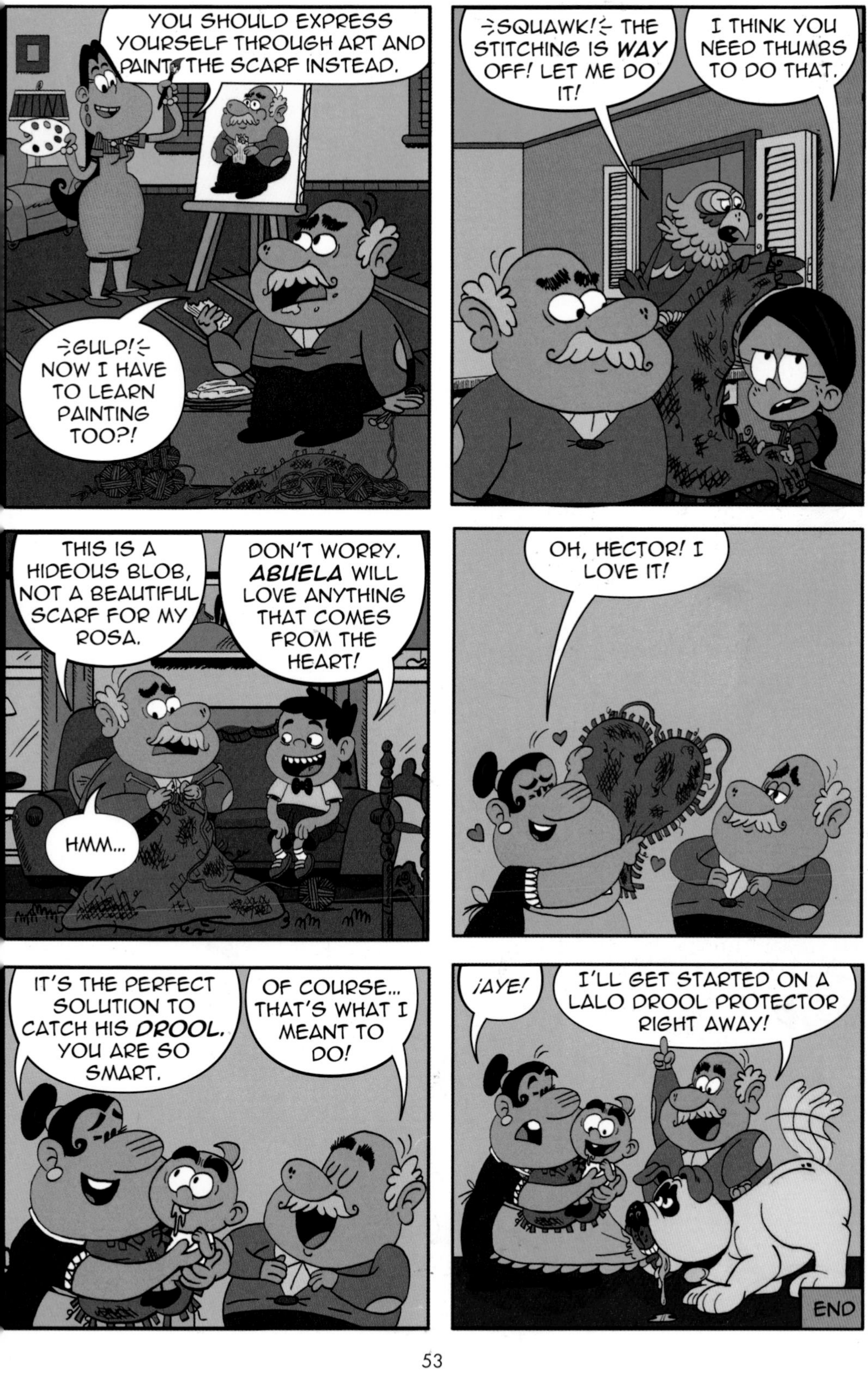
YOU SHOULD EXPRESS YOURSELF THROUGH ART AND PAINT THE SCARF INSTEAD.
⇉GULP!⇇ NOW I HAVE TO LEARN PAINTING TOO?!
⇉SQUAWK!⇇ THE STITCHING IS *WAY* OFF! LET ME DO IT!
I THINK YOU NEED THUMBS TO DO THAT.
THIS IS A HIDEOUS BLOB, NOT A BEAUTIFUL SCARF FOR MY ROSA.
DON'T WORRY. ***ABUELA*** WILL LOVE ANYTHING THAT COMES FROM THE HEART!
HMM...
OH, HECTOR! I LOVE IT!
IT'S THE PERFECT SOLUTION TO CATCH HIS *DROOL*. YOU ARE SO SMART.
OF COURSE... THAT'S WHAT I MEANT TO DO!
¡AYE!
I'LL GET STARTED ON A LALO DROOL PROTECTOR RIGHT AWAY!
END

"THERE'S SOMETHING ABOUT LALO"

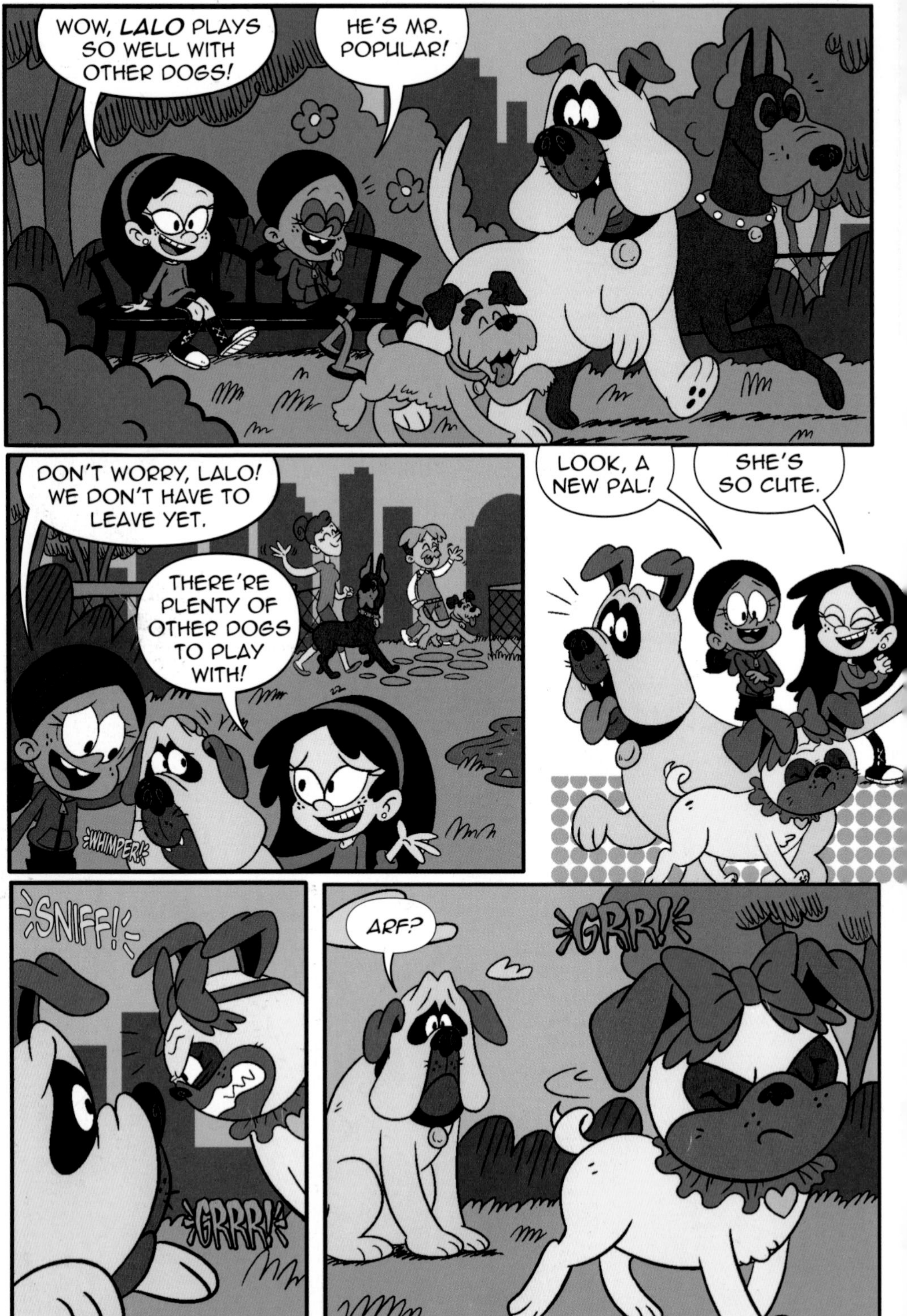
WOW, LALO PLAYS SO WELL WITH OTHER DOGS!
HE'S MR. POPULAR!
DON'T WORRY, LALO! WE DON'T HAVE TO LEAVE YET.
THERE'RE PLENTY OF OTHER DOGS TO PLAY WITH!
WHIMPER!
LOOK, A NEW PAL!
SHE'S SO CUTE.
SNIFF!
GRRR!
ARF?
GRR!

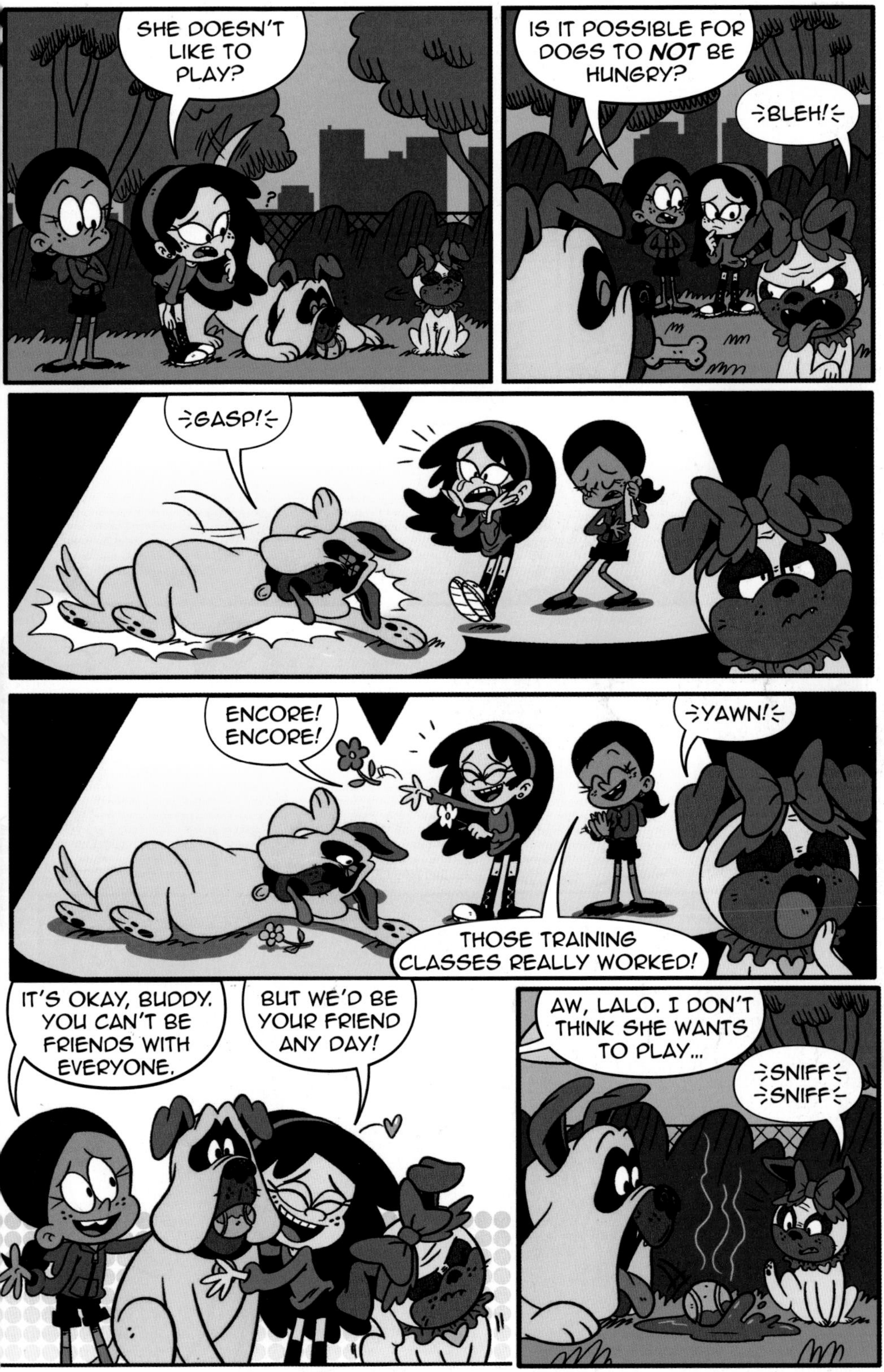
SHE DOESN'T LIKE TO PLAY?
IS IT POSSIBLE FOR DOGS TO NOT BE HUNGRY?
BLEH!
GASP!
ENCORE! ENCORE!
YAWN!
THOSE TRAINING CLASSES REALLY WORKED!
IT'S OKAY, BUDDY. YOU CAN'T BE FRIENDS WITH EVERYONE.
BUT WE'D BE YOUR FRIEND ANY DAY!
AW, LALO. I DON'T THINK SHE WANTS TO PLAY...
SNIFF
SNIFF

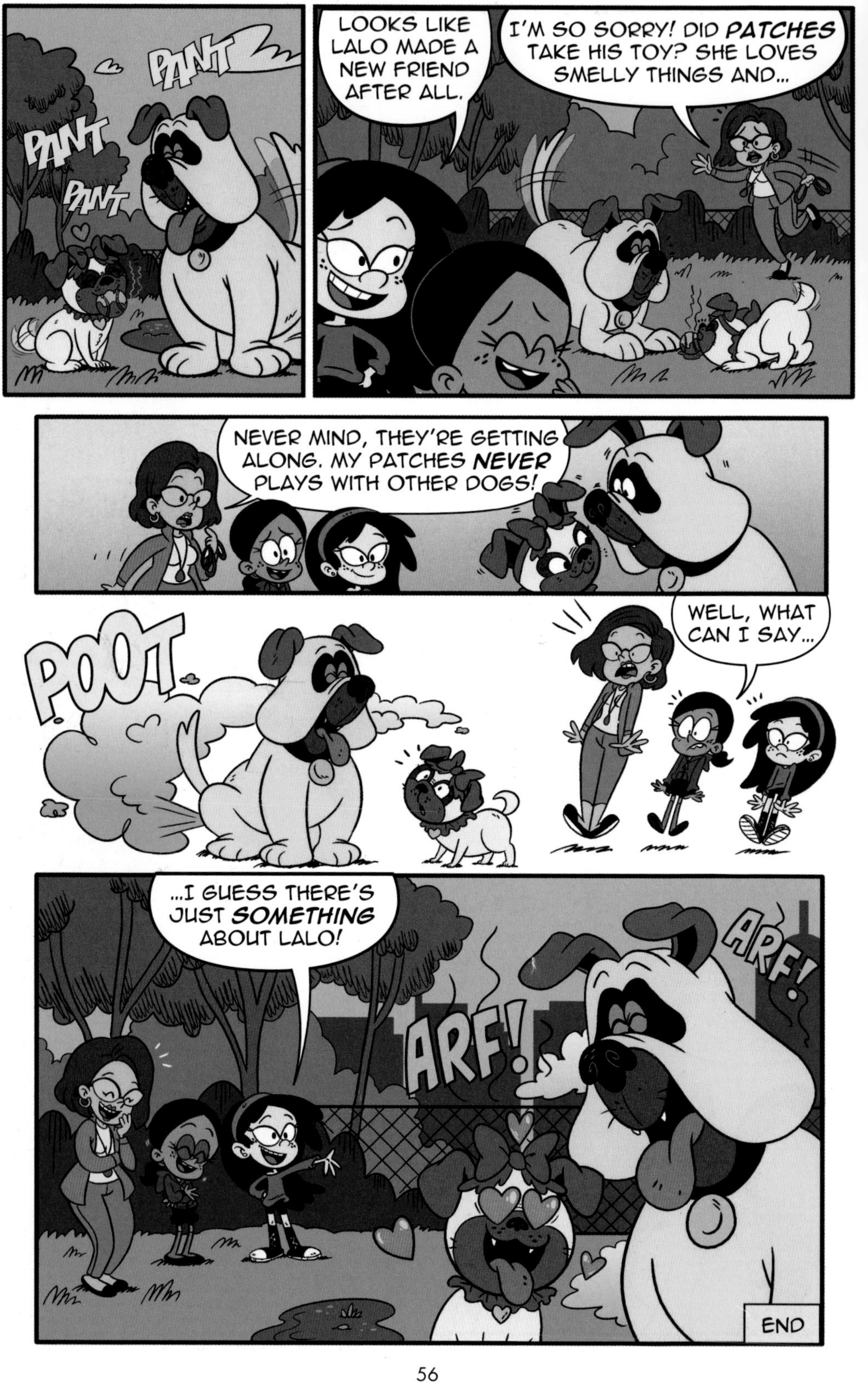
PANT
PANT
PANT
LOOKS LIKE LALO MADE A NEW FRIEND AFTER ALL.
I'M SO SORRY! DID PATCHES TAKE HIS TOY? SHE LOVES SMELLY THINGS AND...
NEVER MIND, THEY'RE GETTING ALONG. MY PATCHES NEVER PLAYS WITH OTHER DOGS!
POOT
WELL, WHAT CAN I SAY...
...I GUESS THERE'S JUST SOMETHING ABOUT LALO!
ARF!
ARF!
END

"FRIENDIVERSARY"

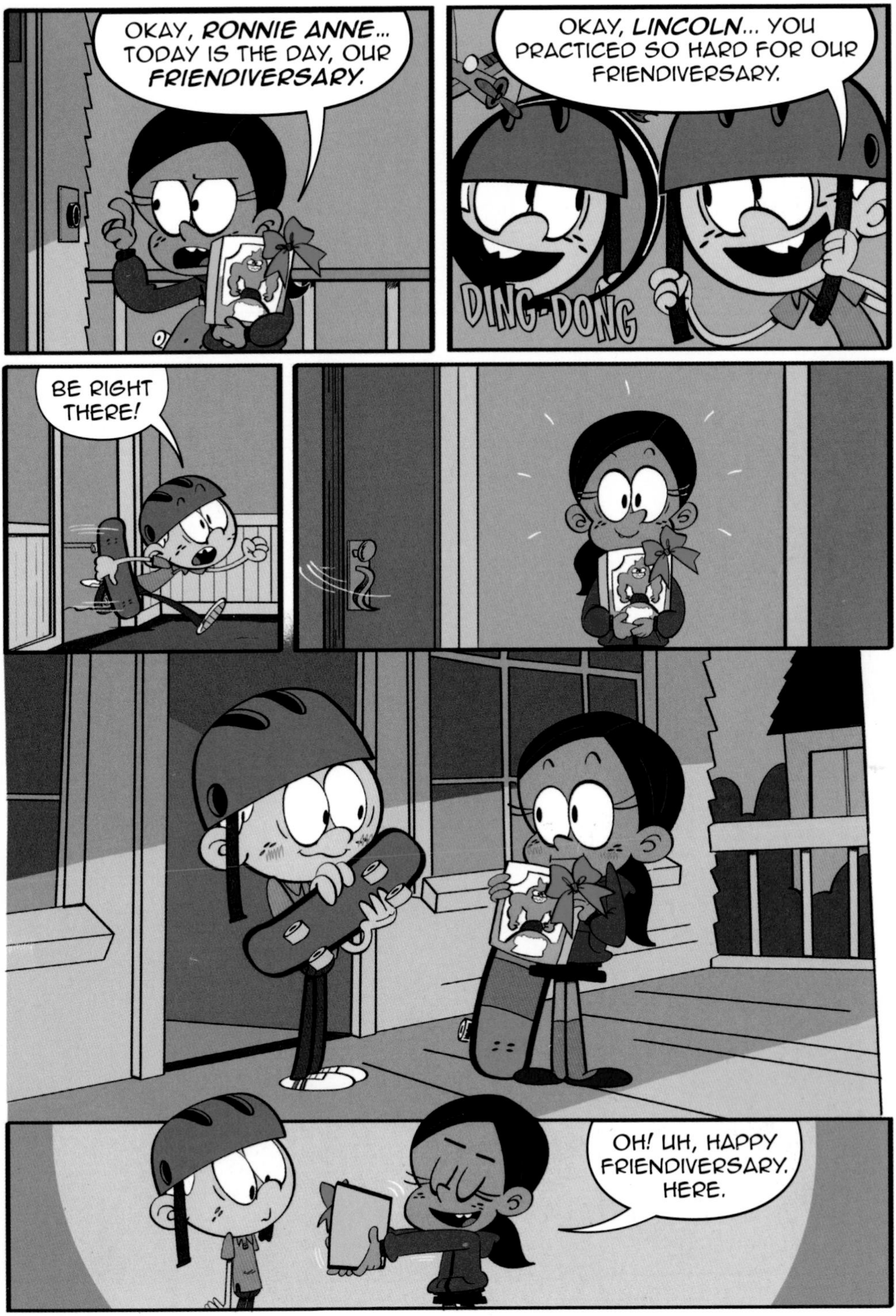
OKAY, RONNIE ANNE... TODAY IS THE DAY, OUR FRIENDIVERSARY.
OKAY, LINCOLN... YOU PRACTICED SO HARD FOR OUR FRIENDIVERSARY.
DING-DONG
BE RIGHT THERE!
OH! UH, HAPPY FRIENDIVERSARY. HERE.

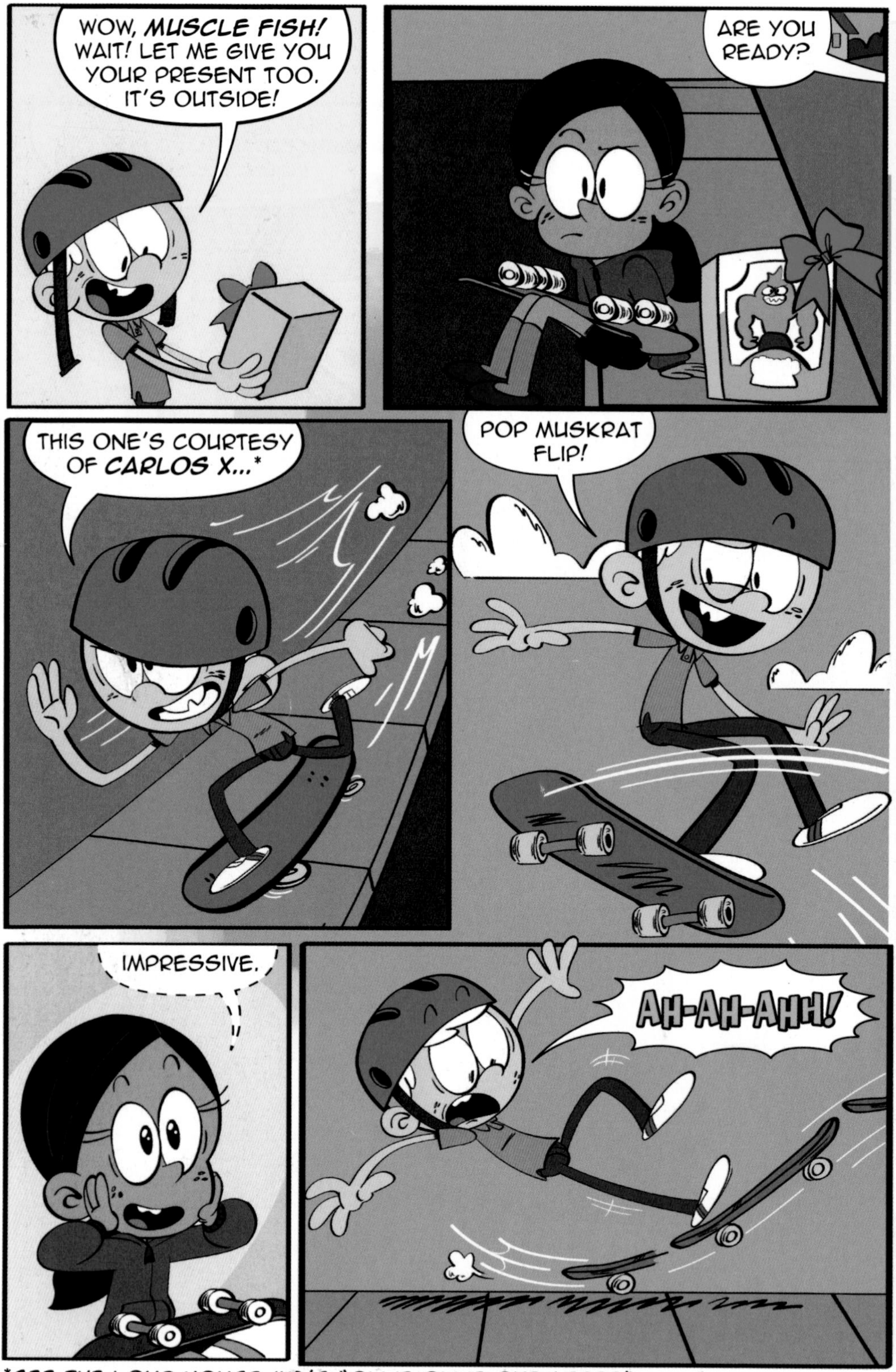
WOW, MUSCLE FISH! WAIT! LET ME GIVE YOU YOUR PRESENT TOO. IT'S OUTSIDE!
ARE YOU READY?
THIS ONE'S COURTESY OF CARLOS X...*
POP MUSKRAT FLIP!
IMPRESSIVE.
AH-AH-AHH!

*SEE THE LOUD HOUSE #12'S "OLLIE, OLLIE OXEN FREE"

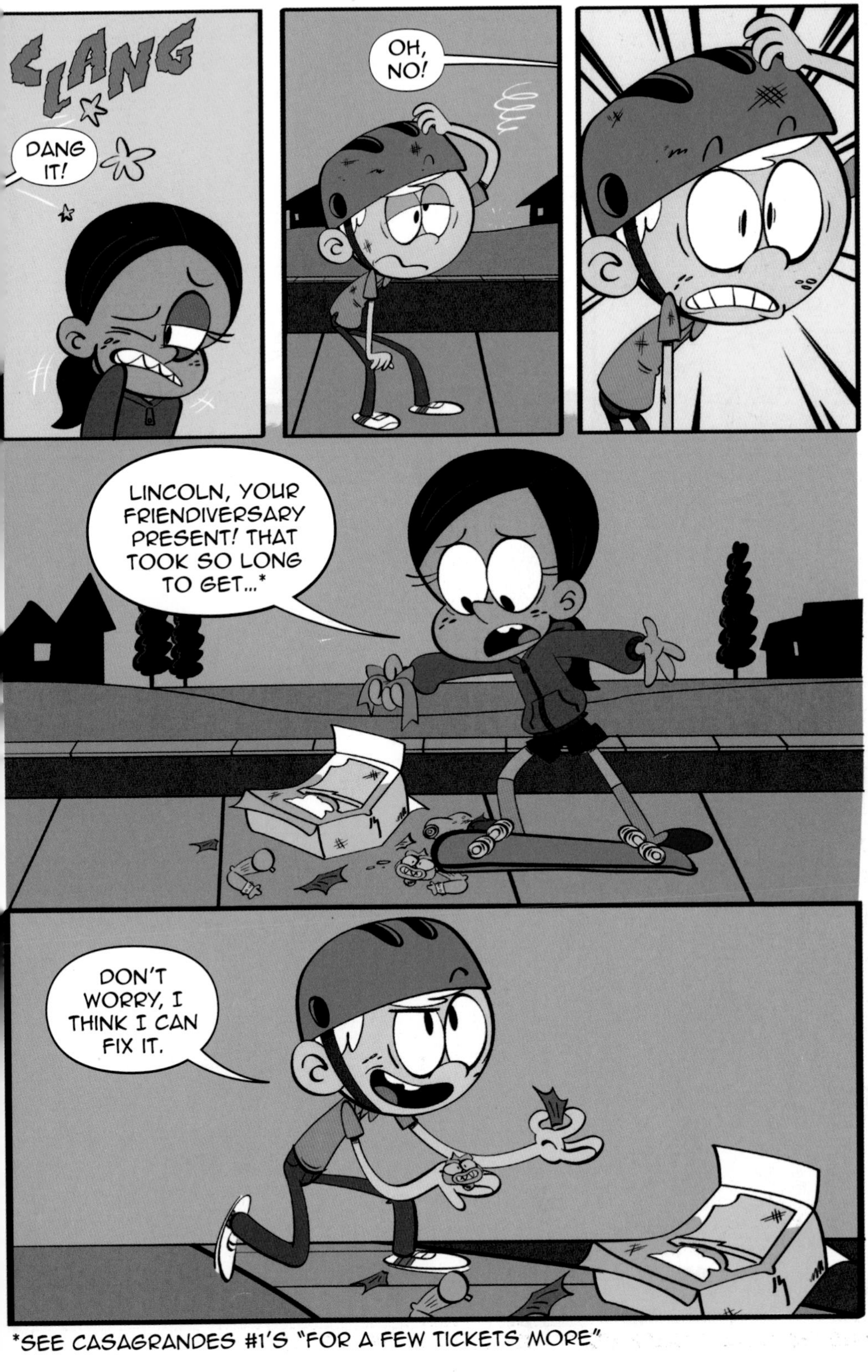
CLANG
DANG IT!
OH, NO!
LINCOLN, YOUR FRIENDIVERSARY PRESENT! THAT TOOK SO LONG TO GET...*
DON'T WORRY, I THINK I CAN FIX IT.

*SEE CASAGRANDES #1'S "FOR A FEW TICKETS MORE"

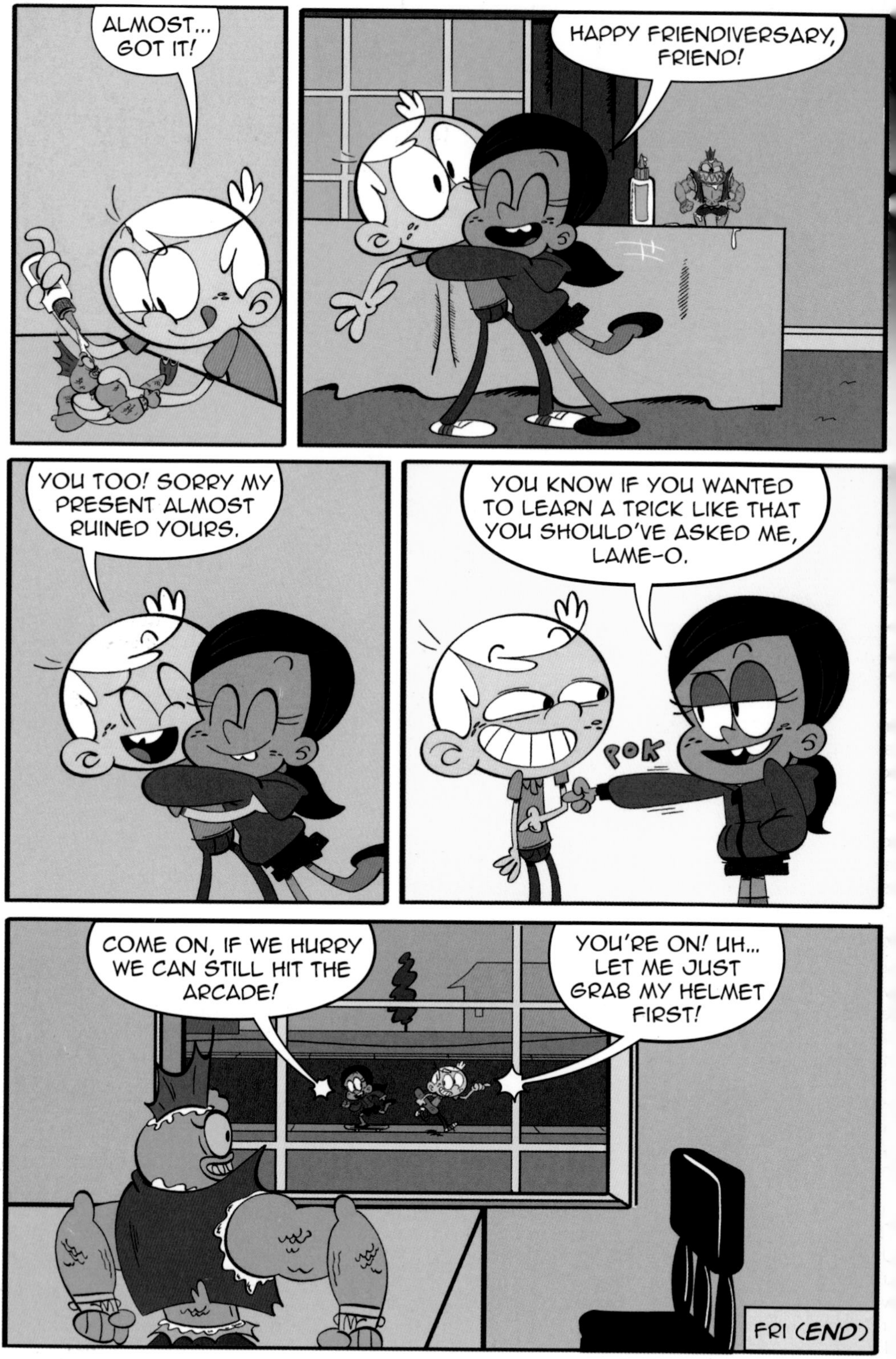
ALMOST... GOT IT!
HAPPY FRIENDIVERSARY, FRIEND!
YOU TOO! SORRY MY PRESENT ALMOST RUINED YOURS.
YOU KNOW IF YOU WANTED TO LEARN A TRICK LIKE THAT YOU SHOULD'VE ASKED ME, LAME-O.
POK
COME ON, IF WE HURRY WE CAN STILL HIT THE ARCADE!
YOU'RE ON! UH... LET ME JUST GRAB MY HELMET FIRST!
FRI (END)

WATCH OUT FOR PAPERCUTZ™

Welcome to THE LOUD HOUSE extra-special, extra-lovable graphic novel "Love Out Loud," from Papercutz, those love-sick souls dedicated to publishing great graphic novels for all ages. I'm Jim Salicrup, Editor-in-Chief and Hopeless Romantic, here to talk about love, Loud-style.

While this special edition of THE LOUD HOUSE is obviously built around the wonderful theme of love, the truth is that you can find examples of love in every volume of THE LOUD HOUSE graphic novels and on the Nickelodeon TV series as well. I'm not just talking about the various characters that are part of couples who are in love with each other, but the love the Loud family clearly has for each other and for their many friends. And it's a good thing that they're so loving—it's difficult enough for most average-sized families to get along, for a family with eleven children, as many of the stories in this graphic novel illustrate, it's quite a challenge!

While we often see those challenges played out here and on TV, one of the reasons things usually work out so well for the Loud family is the love and respect they have for each other. Clearly each child has had the freedom to pursue their own special interests with nothing but love and support coming from their parents, relatives, and friends. What a truly wonderful environment in which to grow up. Everyone is free to be exactly who they want to be, and they're accepted and loved. The same is true for THE CASAGRANDES as well.

I can only hope and wish that everyone who enjoys THE LOUD HOUSE is equally lucky in their lives. Unfortunately, we know that in the real world things are not always quite as wonderful as we wish they were. It's important for each of us to remember that and to do our best to treat everyone like we would like to be treated. It's not always easy, but sometimes just a little bit of kindness can go a long way. For example, if you know someone else who loves THE LOUD HOUSE as much as you, you might offer to share this very graphic novel with that person. It's fun to have a common interest with a friend or family member. It's great to see fans of THE LOUD HOUSE discuss the latest episodes and graphic novels online—even when individuals disagree about specific bits, they're still bound together with a shared love for THE LOUD HOUSE.

While the priority for the creators of THE LOUD HOUSE cartoons and comics is to provide entertaining stories that we hope will make you laugh, we also hope that while you're enjoying THE LOUD HOUSE you also feel the love and know that you're loved too.

Love is love.

Thanks,

Jim

We have two special bonuses that you are sure to love! First, a look at Tyler Kobertstein's creative process putting together the cover for this very volume! Then, a callback to the origins of the Friendiversary, all the way back in ninth THE LOUD HOUSE graphic novel! Enjoy!

STAY IN TOUCH!

EMAIL:	salicrup@papercutz.com
WEB:	papercutz.com
TWITTER:	@papercutzgn
INSTAGRAM:	@papercutzgn
FACEBOOK:	PAPERCUTZGRAPHICNOVELS
FANMAIL:	Papercutz, 160 Broadway, Suite 700, East Wing, New York, NY 10038

Go to papercutz.com and sign up for the free Papercutz e-newsletter!

As a special sweet treat, see the behind-the-scenes process of how this cover came to life by artist TYLER KOBERSTEIN!

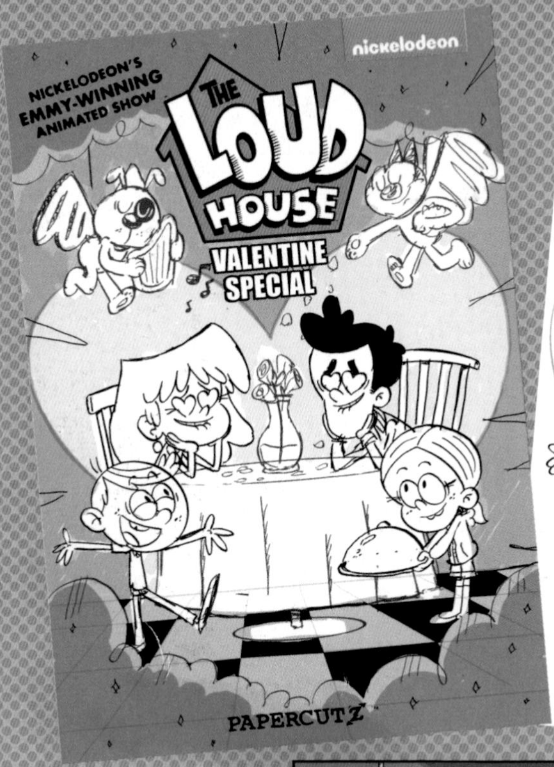
NICKELODEON'S
EMMY-WINNING
ANIMATED SHOW
nickelodeon
THE LOUD HOUSE
VALENTINE SPECIAL
PAPERCUTZ

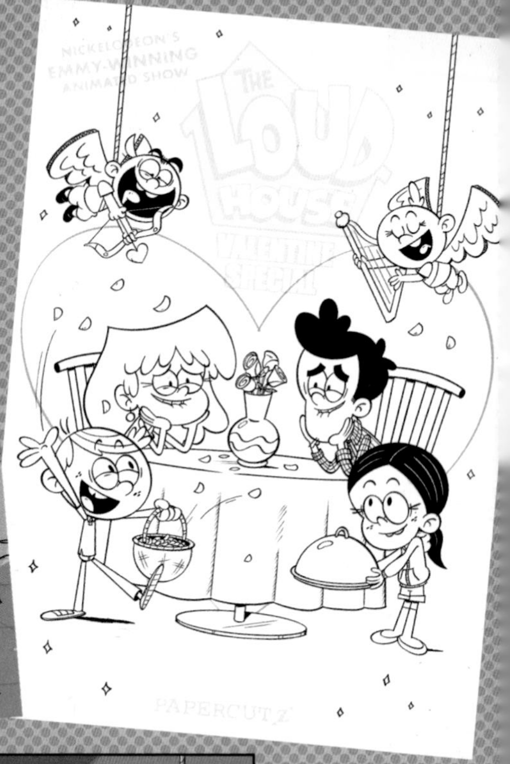
NICKELODEON'S
EMMY-WINNING
ANIMATED SHOW
THE LOUD HOUSE
VALENTINE SPECIAL
PAPERCUTZ

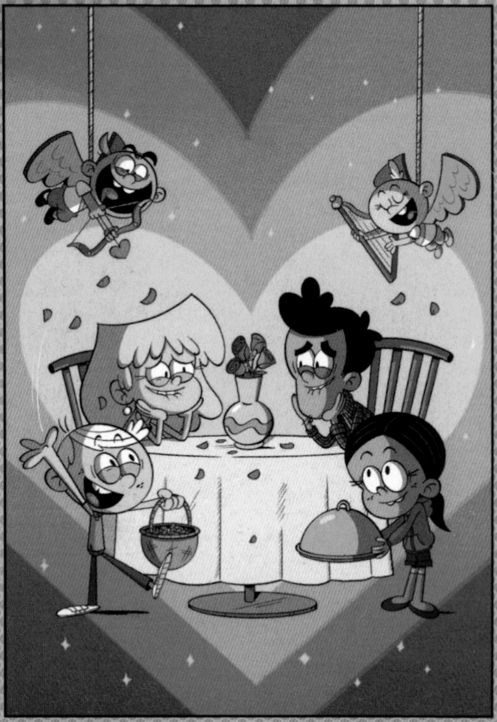

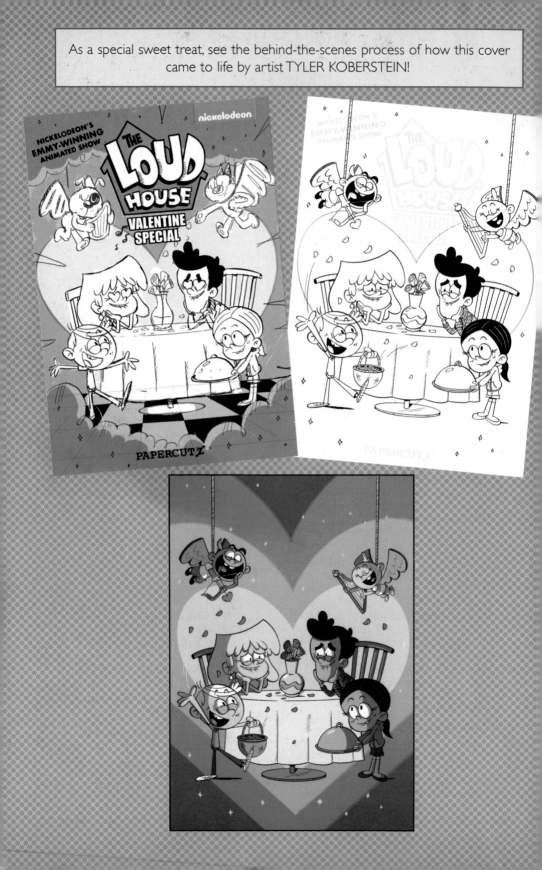

"THE PERFECT GIFT"

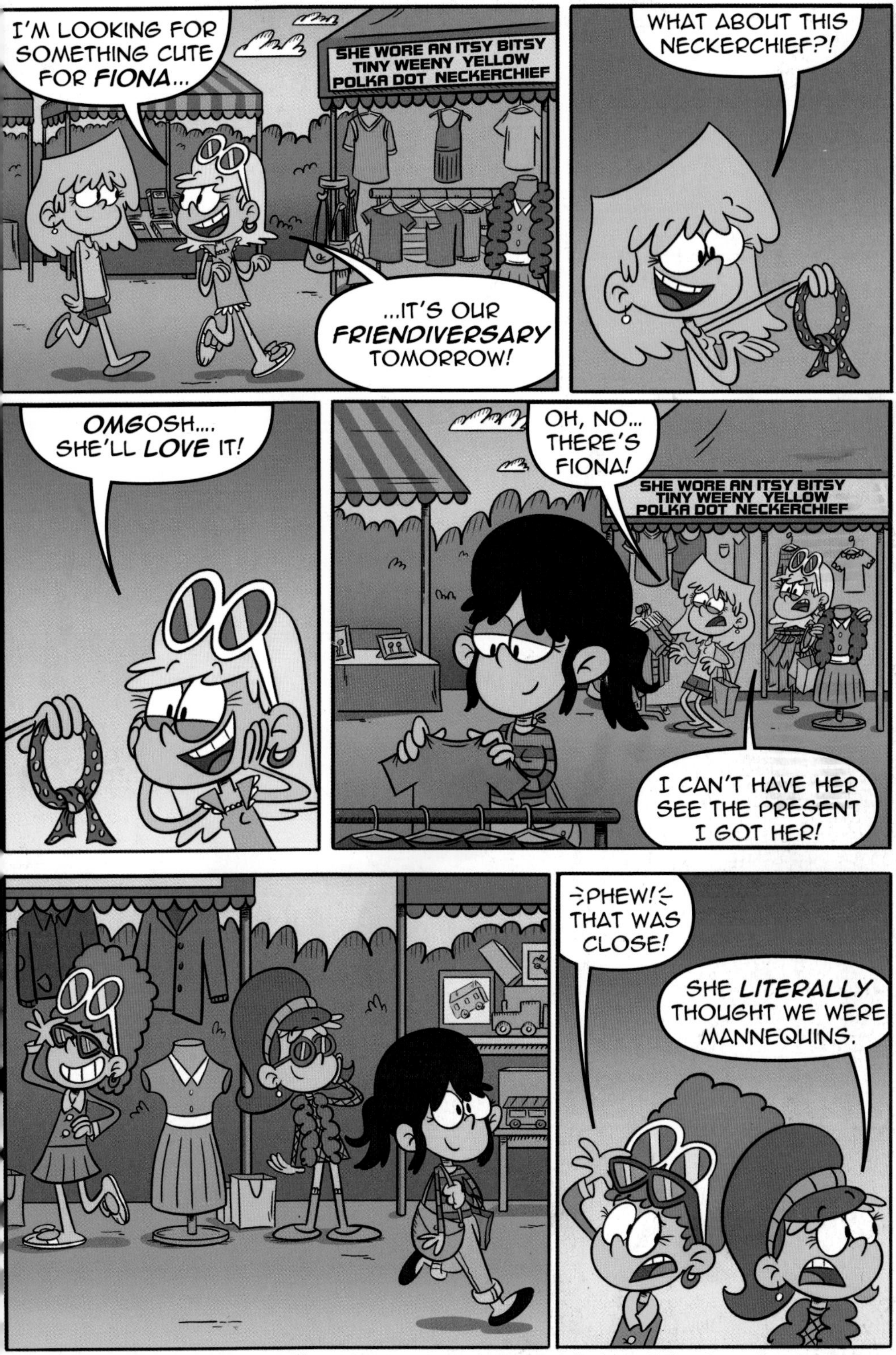
I'M LOOKING FOR SOMETHING CUTE FOR FIONA...
SHE WORE AN ITSY BITSY TINY WEENY YELLOW POLKA DOT NECKERCHIEF
...IT'S OUR FRIENDIVERSARY TOMORROW!
WHAT ABOUT THIS NECKERCHIEF?!
OMGOSH.... SHE'LL LOVE IT!
OH, NO... THERE'S FIONA!
SHE WORE AN ITSY BITSY TINY WEENY YELLOW POLKA DOT NECKERCHIEF
I CAN'T HAVE HER SEE THE PRESENT I GOT HER!
PHEW! THAT WAS CLOSE!
SHE LITERALLY THOUGHT WE WERE MANNEQUINS.

Katie Mattila — Writer • Max Alley — Artist • JayJay Jackson— Colorist • Wilson Ramos Jr. — Letterer

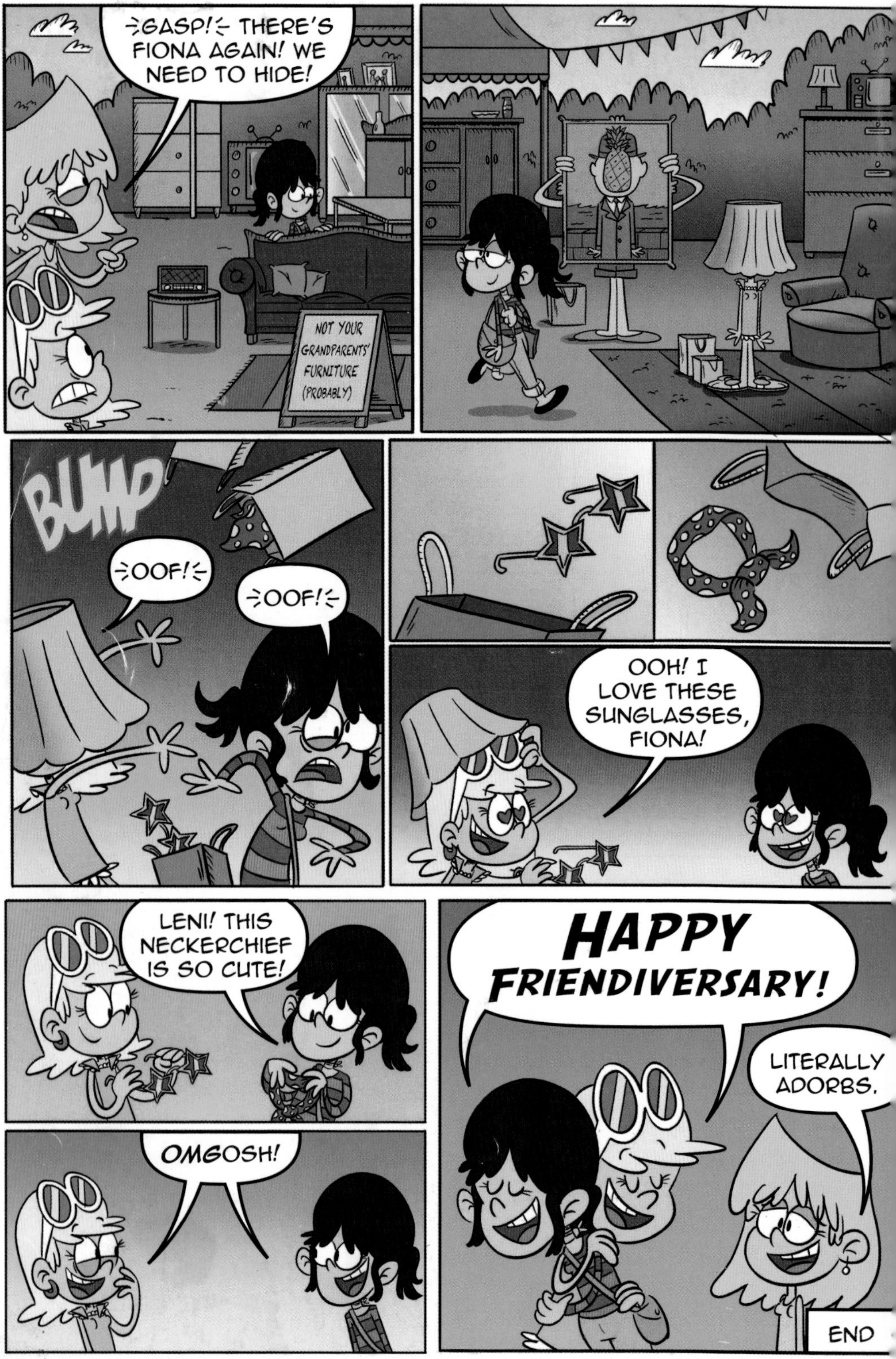

GASP! THERE'S FIONA AGAIN! WE NEED TO HIDE!
NOT YOUR GRANDPARENTS' FURNITURE (PROBABLY)
BUMP
OOF!
OOF!
OOH! I LOVE THESE SUNGLASSES, FIONA!
LENI! THIS NECKERCHIEF IS SO CUTE!
OMGOSH!
HAPPY FRIENDIVERSARY!
LITERALLY ADORBS.
END